In Between

Lynn Burke

In Between

After his stepfather nearly ruins both his family name and business, Damien Fiorenza becomes suspicious of everyone—except for his long-time partner, Ethan Lord. He doesn't trust people in authority, much less the woman who weasels her way into his walled-up heart, alongside his lover of fifteen years.

Ethan dislikes his empathic abilities, especially since they allow him to feel his mother's indifference toward him, her only son. Damien, however, has always made Ethan feel needed, appreciated, and protected—but he can't voice what Ethan is desperate to hear. Falling for their new secretary is unexpected, but she encourages and supports him in ways Damien won't.

Shaylia Bright's father chose his secret family over her and her mother. Ever since, she's striven to be the best she can be, unable to stomach being second best. Although an office romance is taboo, she can't deny the passionate chemistry among the three of them and finds herself drawn to both her bosses.

A dark and deep secret from the past forces Damien to raise his defenses. Haunting revelations tear everyone apart, dooming Shaylia to second best and Ethan to an incomplete life. Wrought with insecurity and stubbornness, can they find the courage to accept parts of their painful past in order to forge a path together toward a happily ever after?

Chapter 1

Damien

"I'm going to open my own gallery." Ethan's voice hinted at hesitation, but I finished pouring my second cup of coffee before turning to acknowledge him.

I leaned on the kitchen counter, my dick tenting my lounge pants at the sight of my partner in his new Armani suit. The lithe swimmer's body beneath the slim-fitted wool had writhed beneath my hold not an hour earlier—one last fuck before I left for an extended business trip to London.

"Why are you bringing this up now?" I asked and sipped as his hazel-eyed gaze flitted to our condo's door then to his fingers fiddling with the top button of his coat.

"Because I know you don't want me to, and I don't want to fight," he said, resignation weighing his tone as he lifted his head and met my gaze.

"That's a shit thing to drop on me this morning," I said, annoyed at his timing, yet still turned on by his hot-as-fuck appearance.

"I figured it would give you a few weeks to accept my decision."

I kept my lips sealed to the rim of my coffee cup and sucked down the black, bitter brew, wishing for a nice Grey Goose on the rocks instead.

"I need to do this for myself, Damien." While I couldn't feel his emotions like he could mine with his empathic abilities, his gaze implored me to understand. "I want to follow my own dreams for once, and I would really like your support."

Dreams of making something of himself in the art world had plagued Ethan since I'd met him our freshman year in college. With opposites attracting and both of us being bi, we'd ended up fucking before the first semester's end. He'd become an addiction I couldn't resist, a softer soul to my hardened one, his gift at feeling my emotions a relief since I didn't know how to communicate them.

When my stepfather had run my grandfather's financial firm into the dust our sophomore year, it had been Ethan who kept me from losing my shit. Riches to rags in a matter of a few hours, my mother and I were blindsided by the man we had both admired and put on a pedestal. He sat in jail for the dozens of counts of fraud he'd been found guilty of. Ethan's financial genius—along with his ability to read people—had been what saved my family's name.

"We're just now getting Fiorenza Financial back to where it was in my grandfather's time," I said, setting my coffee aside and crossing my arms. "I need you."

His wry smile through a dark trimmed beard usually made my balls tighten, but lust lacked in his eyes, diminishing mine. "You *need* me, yes, but do you love me?"

"You're the only one I trust," I answered as I always did when he asked me that question. "I can't even trust my own mother's judgement."

"But if you do trust me, what's stopping you from saying that four-letter word?"

We'd had this conversation countless times. Irked yet again, I fought to keep from huffing in annoyance. "The last person I told that ruined my family name."

We studied one another in silence, something that came much easier for Ethan than me. My heart beat faster in my chest but not out of physical need. Reality bent—shifted beneath my feet as though my life beyond that point would be changed forever. Still, I held my silence, unable to give him what he needed. Even if I'd wanted to tell him the truth of how I cared for him, my tightening throat wouldn't allow my lips movement.

"I've asked you for two things in the past few years," Ethan finally said, resignation lowering his voice once more. "A declaration of your love and support of my dreams. You can't give me either."

"I'm an asshole," I muttered since stating the reality of my personality came easier than putting my emotions into words.

"You are, but I love you." His brow furrowed slightly. "I understand your need for control, Damien. I can *feel* it emanating off you every minute of the goddamn day, but it's only a word."

"We've been together for fifteen years. You know how I feel about you." I grabbed my coffee and strode into the living room, my stomach roiling, tension eating at my brow and shoulders.

Talking about my emotions didn't come easy. Ethan's entrance into my life prior to the bastard almost destroying me and my mother had kept him safe from my cynical thoughts and mistrust. Closer than a brother, closer than blood, Ethan had become a part of me. The one I looked out for when he became overwhelmed by his empathy. The one I held tight when the emotions of others wore his own emotions thin.

"Why can't you just say it?" Ethan asked, following on my heels like a bulldog with its teeth sunk into my skin —something he didn't usually do.

I sat on the leather couch overlooking Boston's skyline, the rising sun hinting at a beautiful summer morning. A fucking *Monday* morning, a few hours before my plane departed, and my partner felt the need to dive into his insecurities, knowing full well I wouldn't be able to voice what he wanted to hear. Pinching the bridge of my nose, I heaved a heavy exhale.

"I would like to have your blessing, Damien." The finality of his tone dropped my heart.

"You're doing this regardless of what I think or say, aren't you?" I asked, turning my head to capture his stare, my hand clenching the mug in fear of the answer I knew rested in his mind.

His chin tipped upward the slightest bit, an act of defiance I would usually enjoy fucking out of him. "Yes."

Lips pressed tight, I turned away, seeking to control my anger, disappointment, and hurt. Losing control over my life and all who had the ability to influence it didn't settle well, and that damn shifting reality beneath me almost buckled my hold on my emotions.

"Maybe it's time for a break."

I jerked my head toward Ethan, a scowl denting my brow as a knife-like ache pierced my chest. "What?"

"A break." He motioned between us. "See other people. Maybe that will help you figure out what your true feelings are for me." A half-snort of laughter I didn't find the least bit amusing puffed past his lips. "I used to love the fact you're able to keep most of your emotions hidden from me, but for the first time, I wish my empath abilities conquered you as well."

I stared at him until he turned away, his shoulders tense and straight, showing a backbone I'd never seen before. Ethan deserved my worship, my goddamn allowance of control, but giving it over festered like a sickness in my head.

"Are you breaking up with me?" I managed to rasp past my dry throat.

Ethan didn't vocalize his thoughts, but a slight shift of one shoulder turned my stomach to stone and narrowed my eyes.

I set my mug on the coffee table in front of me and stood, stalking toward him. He dropped his gaze and shuffled away from me until he hit the wall. Grasping the back of his neck, I squeezed until he winced and wilted in my hold.

"You're fucking breaking up with me?" I growled close to his ear, loving how he caved to my dominance so easily. What a fucking pair we made...

"I-I need more than you're willing—"

I grabbed his flaccid cock with my free hand, stroking him through his slacks. "You groaned my name less than an hour ago while my dick was buried in your ass."

His dick twitched in my hold. "Please," he half-whispered but without the longing that usually coated his voice when I held him in my hand.

"Do you want to date other men, Ethan? Do you want another man's cock shoved down your throat while you kneel before him? Will you beg him like you do me?" I backed off enough to see his face. Eyes clenched shut and lower lip between his teeth, he seemed to fight his natural submission to me.

"Or do you want pussy?" I whispered, my own dick jerking in my pants. We'd shared a few women over the years for fun, but I thought we'd been content with one another. "Is that it, Ethan? You want a wet, willing hole to thrust your dick into? An emotional female you can coddle? Do you need softness to love since I'm such a cold-hearted bastard?"

"Damien." His strangled tone leaked pre-cum from my dick.

"Tell me what you want," I whispered against his ear and bit on his lobe.

"Goddamn you." He pushed away from me with more force than I expected, swallowed, and straightened his suit coat with shaking hands.

Ethan had never pulled or pushed away from me—ever.

I stared, arms at my sides, hands fisting. "You're sending me off to London for a month with this shit between us?"

"I'm sorry, Damien, but I can't go on like this any longer." He turned and strode away, shoulders hunched, but determination in his footfalls. "I need to take care of *me* for a change."

Our condo's door closed behind him with a soft click, and I stared, waiting for him to return and call a late April fool's joke, to tell me he was just busting my balls.

He didn't.

"What the fuck?" I muttered, scrubbing a hand down over my unshaved face. Two days-worth of stubble scraped my palm, and I swore again. Ethan had broken up with me. "*Fuck*." My erection flagged as I moved back to the master bedroom we had shared for over ten years.

Navy-blue rumpled sheets held evidence of our fucking, lube and cum smears only slightly dried. I'd held him down by the neck, staring into his pupil-dominated eyes while fucking him, his hands gently wrapped around my wrists with complete trust—something I thought I'd given him, the one man who deserved it the most from me.

I *had* given him my trust—and he'd yanked the goddamn rug from beneath my feet with one conversation.

Jaw clenched against the pain I remembered all too well, I hopped in the shower, determined to keep my mind on what truly mattered—the deal awaiting me in London. The opening of an overseas office, the expansion that would take Fiorenza Financial from household to global.

Closing the deal in London would be easy for me, but I needed Ethan for the shaping of our business' future since he had a gift for investments and numbers like my grandfather had.

Close the deal.

"And in four weeks," I muttered while drying off, "I'll return and reclaim the man who belongs to me."

Chapter 2

Ethan

Damien insisted on light jazz filtering through the entire office overhead speakers. While subtle, the constant noise atop the emotions of every person I slipped past in the hallway aggravated me to the point I struggled to not rip at my hair and holler for everyone to just calm the fuck down already. The boss would be out of the office for four weeks—the employees should have been upbeat for a Monday morning.

With a murmured greeting to our secretary, Madeline, I hurried into my private office—quiet, thank fuck.

I'd wanted to talk to Damien weeks earlier when I asked him if he would attend an upcoming art show with me. He'd declined—too busy—and I couldn't handle further disappointment at that time. The nerve to tell him of what I planned to do had escaped me.

Why the hell it spilled from my mouth that morning, I didn't know. I'd had no intention of placing a wedge between us, especially with him heading overseas for four weeks. I figured if a breakup happened, it would be his doing since my mind was set on doing something selfish, something solely for myself for the first time since meeting him.

But a weight had lifted off my shoulders, one that had been slowly burying me for months. Damien had been *it* for me for over fifteen years, but the sudden freedom from his dominance created a giddiness I wasn't sure how to express. I wasn't sure what to make of it. My love for him hadn't faded, but I knew I needed more, something he wouldn't give me.

My dream lay on the horizon, offering happiness, and yet losing the most precious thing in my life ached my heart. Looking at Damien always made me think of a mirrored image as though the other half of my soul resided inside him even though we were polar opposites personality-wise. Submitting to his more dominant nature was like breathing for me. I longed to please him in all things, in any way he wished—and my greatest wish was for him to feel the same.

Being an empath, I knew how he felt, and while he considered my need to hear those three words insecurity, I merely wanted him finally to acknowledge he *could* love again, could trust completely. He needed to take that step for his own sense of self, to become a better version of himself I knew laid inside.

I blew out a breath and sank into my office chair, my back to the brightly lit window, the rising sun promising a new beginning. My gaze flitted to the right and the door which linked my office to Damien's. He would be gone for four weeks, plenty of time for me to focus on moving on with my life as I'd told him—looking at the available rental properties I'd found online that could be converted to a gallery and possibly, sign a lease.

Enough paintings sat in our guest room—boxed up and unloved, in need of bringing joy to people's homes—outfitting a small gallery wouldn't be an issue. I had already spoken with a few of my contacts in the art world, going so far as to offer retail space for commission once I made the final steps in making my dream come true.

My phone's intercom buzzed through the plans flitting through my head. I leaned forward and hit the button while grabbing a couple Necco Wafers from the half-eaten pack on my desk. "Yes, Madeline?"

"The new secretary from the temp agency is here."

Shit. I crunched down on a white wafer, cursing Damien for leaving me—once again—with greeting the newest employee, to feel them out. Miss Bright was only a temporary fix until we found someone worthy of filling the shoes of our other secretary who had been forced to retire early due to health issues.

"Send her in." Standing, I buttoned my coat and stretched my neck, side to side.

Emotional overload time—every new hire, every new trainee, or seasoned financial advisor showed up their first day with enough internal stress and nerves to wreck an empath like me.

That night, I wouldn't have Damien's arms to comfort me.

My chest ached, but I put on a fake smile and made my way forward to greet Miss Bright as the door pushed inward.

Holy fucking shit.

I nearly stumbled over my damn feet as she slipped into my office, her bright blue eyes ensnaring me the second our gazes locked. Long, dark lashes blinked, her brows arched, as dark as the pulled-back hair sitting atop her head in a messy bun. High cheekbones blushed pink, the same color as her glossed lips, and my smile came easier.

Damien had asked if I'd wanted an emotional female to coddle, someone softer, and even though that hadn't been my intention, Shaylia Bright fit the bill perfectly. While her emotions didn't swarm over me, her insecurities made me want to wrap her in my arms and kiss them away, pamper and pet her until she laid lax against me.

I cleared my throat and extended my hand. "Miss Bright, I'm Ethan Lord."

"Hello." Her husky, low tone twitched my dick—the first woman to do so without Damien in close proximity.

The second our fingers brushed, energy pulsed up my arm, tightening my chest. Our hands clasped, and my pulse thudded in my ears as I lost myself in the clear ocean of her eyes. Her nervousness didn't turn my stomach as people's usually did. Her excitement amped my own, making me feel connected to her, a complete stranger.

I grinned for real, and her smile weakened my goddamn knees. The thought of asking her if she wanted to run away together to some deserted island in the Pacific ran through my head, but I dropped her hand and tore my focus off her face before making a fool of myself.

"Please, sit." I settled into my chair, trying like hell to collect myself, shuffling around files on my desk. "There's nothing to be nervous about," I found myself saying, glancing up as she shifted on her chair.

She lifted a slender hand, reaching to tuck a wayward strand of hair behind her ear as she pressed her lips together.

"I'm sure you're going to make us proud." I smiled again, hoping to ease her a bit.

Her gaze settled on my face, her head tilting to the side. "You're very intuitive, Mr. Lord."

Fuck, that voice. I fought the need to adjust myself in my slacks.

"I'm an empath," I blurted. "And please, call me Ethan." While I didn't usually broadcast my abilities in such a way, I wanted Shaylia to know me—inside and out.

The image of Damien flashed in my head—the look in his eyes as he'd fucked me that morning—but I pushed thoughts of him from my head, determined to focus on *me* for a change.

"Then I insist you call me Shaylia." She offered a small and somewhat shy smile while easing back in her chair, her shoulders relaxing as she folded her hands on her lap.

"You came highly recommended, and your credentials are impressive," I said, flipping through her file. When she didn't respond, I glanced up to find her studying her hands.

"I'm sure you're wondering why I'm with a temp agency rather than searching for a full-time job."

"Yes." I sat back and waited, allowing her time to gather her thoughts even though I felt sure she'd rehearsed the coming speech a dozen times.

She lifted her head and held my gaze. "My previous employer sexually assaulted me, and even though I brought charges against him, his wealth and status afforded him a non-guilty plea."

"I'm sorry," I murmured as her hurt over the betrayal of trust slid over me with the stench of sewage sludge.

Her chin tilted upward, a glint in her eyes daring me to delve deeper into her past.

I flipped her file closed and settled back in my chair. "I promise you'll be treated with the utmost respect while working here, Shaylia. And I hope if you ever feel threatened in any way, you'll come to me immediately, seeing as how I'm a master at reading deception and finding the truth through one's emotions." My lips tilted up, more in an irritated smile, rather than in joy over that fact.

"Mr. Fiorenza expects integrity from all of his employees," I continued, "so you needn't worry about encountering such treatment while working for us."

Shaylia blinked slowly, her focus dropping to my mouth and jerking back up to my eyes. The pink staining her cheeks darkened, and my dick twitched again. The sexual energy between us couldn't be ignored, but I had promised her a professional atmosphere for her duration. Nothing would make me break her trust as her last boss had done.

Chapter 3

Shaylia

Ethan Lord's low, soothing tone shivered my skin with every word leaving his full lips, and although my body warmed at the clean scent of him—like softened dryer sheets twice used—I found myself relaxing.

Sexual awareness, something I hadn't expected nor wanted in a new work place, had woken with a vengeance the second his hazel-green eyes peered into mine as though reading right down to the tips of my toes jammed into my heels.

I fought to keep from shifting, pressing my thighs tightly together beneath my pencil skirt, especially once he revealed himself an empath. Could he read my thoughts? Could he feel my attraction to him? He seemed a man more self-aware than any I'd met or dated. His kindness, his sincerity, drew me in with a steady tug, one while pleasant, I did *not* wish to become ensnared in.

I'd learned that lesson once before, and office romance ranked first on my no-no list. Along with giving my heart freely, only to be lied to and left for someone better. My smile wobbled as I struggled to push my past where it belonged—behind me—even though his continued stare warmed me through.

"I appreciate your kindness, Ethan," I finally managed to respond to his assurance of the safe environment I found myself in.

We chatted lightly for a few moments about expectations and what all my job entailed, every passing moment entrenching me more in the fantasy of finding a man such as him, one I could lose myself in.

As the VP of Fiorenza Financial, and by the looks of his carefully groomed appearance and expensive suit, Ethan was way beyond my reach, anyway. A sweet man, but one who would wish for something better than me, a mere secretary desperate to prove herself worthy.

Office romance, I reminded myself again as he smiled, my chest aching the slightest bit. I glanced around his sanctuary, needing a break from his all-seeing eyes.

Abstract art, something I knew nothing about, hung on the walls. Some in softly smudged muted tones reminded me of contentment and happiness, others in boldly stroked lines as though full of anger and annoyance. A myriad of emotion caught on canvas…

I suddenly realized what I studied. My attention flitted back toward Ethan. "You paint others' emotions, don't you?"

He blushed the most gorgeous shade of pink above his trimmed beard and glanced away, showing insecurity I wouldn't expect from such a man.

"It's how I deal with the influx," he said, his voice small.

"You're truly remarkable. Truly," I repeated, gaining the connection between our eyes once more. "You're wasting your talent on a desk job."

His face fell as the words spewed from my lips.

"I-I'm sorry, I shouldn't have said that." I clenched my hands and swallowed.

"I actually have plans to open my own gallery."

"I think that's wonderful!" My smile returned full force at his admission, a woman he'd only just met. "Everyone should pursue their passions."

He studied my face, light returning to his eyes along with his soft smile that woke butterflies in my stomach. "What are your passions, Shaylia?"

A loaded question, one that rooted out the secret parts inside me, but I felt compelled to share the truth with the first man to interest me in years.

"To be the best I can be," I said, my voice hushed while sharing my secret. "To prove there are loyal and trustworthy people on this earth."

"I sense something weighty drives you," he replied, his gaze intense as he leaned forward the slightest bit.

"Yes, but it's a long story, one that began long before the sexual assault at my previous job."

I swore our hearts connected as though we *saw* one another. No barrier existed between us, mere strangers tossed into each other's lives—even if only temporarily.

"Well." He took one of his cards from its holder on his desk, grabbed a pen, and jotted a number down on the back while I eyed the partial sleeve of Necco Wafers on his desk. "I've got a great ear should you ever wish to talk."

"As an empath, I expect you get an earful even when you don't want it."

"More often than not." He chuckled lightly and held out his card. "But that's what an empath's purpose is—to help people."

His eyes didn't hold any joy over his statement, and I wondered how much he hated that part of himself.

"Thank you." I accepted the card from his outstretched hand, our brushing fingers shivering my skin once more.

"Of course."

"Candy for breakfast?" I asked with a smile, motioning toward the wafers, trying like hell to focus on something other than the growing tingle between my thighs.

"If it's Necco Wafers, yes."

We shared a quiet laugh, and I exited his office a few moments later, totally crushing on the VP of Fiorenza Financial.

Twice before the end of the day, Ethan exited his office, and I caught myself staring at his broad shoulders and the slim fit of his slacks hugging muscular legs. I wondered at the ass hidden beneath his suit coat, thoughts of it flexing beneath my heels, heating me to the point of embarrassment. Both times Ethan caught my eye, smiling as though attempting to ease the nervousness eating away at my stomach.

Madeline, their other secretary, wasn't one for office gossip, thank goodness. I'd had enough of that at my last job, and I didn't tend toward nosiness, anyway.

If I proved myself in the six weeks of my time with their firm, perhaps they would consider hiring me full-time, something I never expected to find after my last job. What office would want a secretary who had accused her boss of sexual misconduct? Especially when he'd been found not guilty after an outside investigation?

The reminder of my past worsened the anxiety eating away at my insides, and I fought to focus on the paperwork in front of me as five o'clock neared. Madeline had left moments earlier, and my back and eyes were ready for a break.

"Shaylia?"

I jerked my head up to find Ethan looming over my desk. "Hi, Ethan." I returned his smile and swallowed, feeling like an utter moron for the red that had to stain my cheeks.

He glanced around the reception area before meeting my gaze again. "I'm pursuing my passion," he said, keeping his voice low enough, I had to strain to hear him. "I'm going to look at a property tonight."

"Oh! That's wonderful!" Pure, genuine happiness for him filled me, tugging my lips upward.

"Thanks." He glanced away again, sheepish and shy, a similar tint to his cheeks that I felt on my own. "It's … uh … not common knowledge, and I'd like to keep it that way."

"I'm honored you told me." Still smiling like an idiot with stars probably in my eyes, I stared up at him.

"You're a kind soul, Shaylia." He studied my face, the intensity of his gaze dampening my panties. "I'm happy to have you here. I hope we'll be good friends."

"I'd like that too."

He glanced down at my lips before jerking his gaze away. "I'm off. Have a good evening."

"I hope the property is exactly what you're looking for, Ethan."

After a quick goodbye, he hurried toward the elevators, my stare once more latched onto his backside. I jerked my focus away as he stepped into the elevator. Temptation to glance back to see if he watched me almost won, but I focused on my computer screen instead. The elevator door swished shut, and I sighed, slumping in my chair. A total hottie, shy and sweet... Falling would be wicked easy and totally wrong.

I told myself that truth continuously while driving up Route 1, Boston fading in my rearview mirror. Even once changed into comfy clothes and sitting with an after-dinner glass of white wine, my mind lingered on Ethan. I wanted to text him to ask about the property he'd gone to look at but chewed the inside of my lip to death over doing so.

"He gave you his card," I muttered to myself, flipping the rectangular paper over in my hand to read the word "Cell" and the numbers he'd jotted down in a precise line. I told myself it was purely out of friendship while adding him as a contact into my phone, not any sort of effort to take things beyond where they ought to as employer and employee. Once saved, his number proved too much a temptation, and I clicked the text button alongside his number.

Me: **Hi, it's Shaylia. I'm sorry for bothering you, but I'm dying to know if the property was everything you've been dreaming of.**

I hit "send" before chickening out and nibbled on the corner of my thumb nail ... waiting. My phone dinged before a minute passed.

Hot Boss: **It's perfect. I signed the lease!**

A squeal escaped me as my fingers flew over the screen.

Me: **I think it's awesome you're doing this for yourself.**

I nibbled a bit more as the three dots blinked and blinked. Was I being too forward? Crossing a line?

What if it made him think it was me who instigated the whole mess at my last job?

"Damnit," I muttered to myself before taking a big swallow of wine.

The text ding heaved my heart into my throat.

Hot Boss: **It means a lot you remembered, or cared, for that matter.**

My anxiety fled, and a million other thoughts began to run through my head, most about considering telling him I did care—more than I ought to as his employee and having just met him. An offer to help out painting, setting up the gallery, hell, any little thing he needed wouldn't be proper, so I went with what a new friend would say.

Me: **Best of luck in this new adventure.**

Along with a smiling emoji, he sent back: **I don't remember the last time I was this excited about something.**

Feeling like one myself, I texted, **Kid in a candy store?**

Hot Boss: **One shoving Necco Wafers in his mouth!**

I laughed out loud and sent him a smiley of my own.

Hot Boss: **Thank you for your encouragement, Shaylia. I really appreciate it.**

Sighing, I typed the only thing I *should.*

Me: **Enjoy the rest of your evening. I'll see you tomorrow.**

Hot Boss: **I'm looking forward to it.**

My heart flipped like a toddler attempting her first cartwheel.

Me: **Me, too.**

I hit send before I thought better of saying such a thing.

Chapter 4

Damien

Almost two weeks passed, and even though I'd made headway in the negotiations the first couple of days, I hated that Ethan didn't sit beside me in every meeting. I owned the company, but my right-hand's absence hurt when I finally signed my name with a flourish, closing the deal of the century as far as I was concerned.

Fiorenza Financial's London branch in my hands, I dove into our business plan, every to-do list precise with steps put together by my organized partner, the one I couldn't do without.

I spent the second week meeting with over a dozen brokers and financial advisors we'd made contact with over the previous couple of months, once it looked like the deal would go through. Again, the loss of Ethan for such meetings made me realize how much I depended on him, how much I needed him to help me wade through potential employees.

I sprawled on the bed in the flat I'd rented for four weeks, staring at the ceiling as the TV evening news droned on in the background. My chest fucking ached. I wanted to give Ethan his space, but I missed his voice. I missed his skin against mine in our bed. I missed his breath against my chest when lying together, our bodies sated and sweaty.

I missed the quiet contentment, the rightness of having him by my side.

"Fuck." I scrubbed a hand down my face, my dick swelling at the thought of him. Grasping the base of my hardening dick through my lounge pants, I grabbed my cell off the bed stand and dialed his number.

"Hello."

My lips twitched up as his familiar, low tone caressed my ear. "Hey. How are you?"

"Good. You?"

Ethan tended toward short and sweet over the phone, but he sounded distant—and not just from being across the pond.

"Doing well," I said, closing my eyes and dropping my hold on my wilting dick. "The deal is closed, and I've been meeting with the potential employees we spoke with over the phone."

"How's that going for you?" Ethan sounded bored.

My brow furrowed, and I swallowed back my disappointment. "Good. I've hired six of the twelve. I even interviewed a secretary."

"Mmm."

My stomach twisted. "How are things at home?"

"I signed a lease."

I popped my eyelids open and blinked twice while processing what he'd said. "For an art gallery?"

"Yes."

My frown returned full force, but short of cursing, no other words came to mind.

Ethan's heaved exhale came through, loud and clear. "The first property I looked at turned out to be perfect, and I couldn't pass up the opportunity."

"Well, that's good." I fought to keep my tone level. I wondered if he felt my anger and disappointment over the line.

"It is."

Unsure what to say, I kept quiet, my brain in a combative war over what he'd done, the finality of what it meant for Fiorenza Financial—for us.

"I've got another call coming in," Ethan murmured but with more life in his voice than the previous couple of minutes. "I'll talk to you later."

He fucking hung up—without waiting for me to say goodbye.

"What the fuck?" I stared at my cell, completely baffled by his very non-Ethan ways. My stomach knotted, and the knife-like stab in my chest winced my face.

Ethan had been on my mind twenty-four-seven while I'd been away from home, and he'd hung up on me like I didn't mean jack shit to him after fifteen fucking years.

He really dumped me. For fucking real.

The man I entrusted my heart to had left me. I'd been victimized once again—letting my guard down, trusting, and allowing someone else power over my heart.

I hopped off the bed and yanked on a pair jeans, my mind set on the bar downstairs and a good vodka on the rocks. Hell, maybe I wouldn't be the only lonely, hurting soul in need of a little edification and ego boost.

A nice button-down and loafers donned, and I was out the door, my stride steady, determination to numb my mind and the ache in my chest spurring me onward.

Light jazz played softly in the dimly lit bar area as I scanned its length from the open doorway. Two couples cozied together, their heads bent toward one another. Jaw clenched, I noted the two men and one woman at the far end—all seemingly alone.

One of the men, a blond, wasn't shy about checking me out, but the thought of another dick, of male lips and hands that didn't belong to Ethan, turned my empty stomach.

The woman at the far end of the bar stared into her glass, stirring the remnants of her drink with a cocktail straw, her shoulders slumped. She had blonde hair as well, but hers brushed her shoulders, stick straight with blunt bangs across her forehead. A pencil skirt hugged her ass and thighs, and the dip of her waist couldn't have been more than the span of my hands.

My dick took an interest, twitching for a female for the first time in years. Need for companionship, need for physical touch took me down the bar's length until I stood beside her.

"You look like you could use another drink," I murmured, bending close enough to her personal space she would know I spoke to her.

She tilted her head back, her golden brown eyes peering up at me, filled with the same type of emotion I experienced. Her gaze flicked down over me, then back up, her attempted smile failing.

"Yeah, I could. Looks like you could use one too."

Two fucking souls bonded by pain.

"This seat taken?" I motioned toward the empty stool beside her.

"No," she replied, continuing to study my face.

"I'm Damien," I said, sitting down and holding out my hand.

"Adrienne." Her smooth palm slid against mine, and I smiled as my dick thickened, and her lips parted on a small intake of breath.

The bartender approached, and I ordered my vodka along with another of whatever Adrienne drank. He hooked us up before meandering away, and I angled to face my conquest for the night.

Go with a cheesy pickup or go straight for the goods?

"Here on business?" I asked instead of either thought, having noted her American accent. I sipped my drink, holding her stare.

"Yes."

"Alone?"

"Yes." She sipped again, her gaze calculating, a glint growing in her eyes. "Well, I was until this morning. My ... uh ... co-worker flew home a few days early."

I leaned onto the bar. "Is that a good thing?"

"I think it might be." Her intense study would shift any other man on his stool, but intimidation didn't happen easily for me. "Are you here on business?" she asked.

"Yes."

"You're from Boston."

I swigged down some vodka. "That obvious, huh?"

"I always thought the Boston accent was sexy as hell."

One of my eyebrows lifted as I smirked. "Is that a fact?"

"Mmm." She sipped from her tiny straw, licking her plump lower lip as she set her drink back on the bar.

Fuck, her lips would look good around my cock. Gaze still on her mouth, I swirled my drink, clinking the ice together. "Ever pahk yah car in Hahvahd Yahd?"

Her lips twitched—and she let out a small laugh.

In like Flynn. Grinning, I downed the rest of my vodka and flagged down the bartender.

I'd forgotten how good a woman felt under my hands, how soft, how curvy. Well on our way to being drunk, we stumbled into the elevator. The second the doors slid shut, encasing us in a world of quiet metal, I yanked her around, my fist in her hair, my back pressing her chest into the wall. While I wouldn't allow myself to taste her lips, I wanted to taste every other inch of her lush body. Sliding my nose up her neck, I breathed in the scent of candy—sweet watermelon or apple, I couldn't tell.

I pressed my aching dick into her lower back, snaking my hand around her front, rubbing my palm down over the swell of her pubic bone. "Tell me what you want, Adrienne," I murmured against her ear, feeling generous for a change.

She pressed into my hand with a whimper, her back arching, head tilted to the side to allow me better access to the smooth paleness of her neck.

"I want you to fuck me, but just for tonight."

"Mmm." My dick jerked at the thought of wet, willing pussy, but I didn't have a single rubber on me or in my room. "Any chance you have a condom in that bag?"

Adrienne jerked her head up and down, and the elevator dinged.

"One rule," I said against her ear before backing off. "No kissing."

"I'm good with that."

I stepped away, allowing her to turn. She peered up at me, pupils dominating the brown of her eyes, a sexy smirk tilting her lips. The door slid open, and I laced my fingers through hers, leading her to my room.

Thoughts of Ethan slid through my drunken conscience, but I pushed him to the back of my mind. I was determined to enjoy my first sexual encounter without him in over fifteen years.

Adrienne followed willingly, and within minutes of the flat's door closing behind us, I gave the lonely woman what she wanted.

I'd wanted to fuck the heartache away, but it was Ethan's name my thoughts groaned while filling the condom.

Chapter 5

Ethan

I sat on the couch I'd ordered for my gallery, eyeing the empty, newly painted walls. Boxes of artwork sat in the back room, along with the few other pieces of furniture I had delivered earlier that morning.

Satisfaction coursed through me, pure happiness at my dreams coming to fruition, but in the next moment, disappointment over not having anyone to share my joy dragged my lips back down to a flat line.

I'd spoken to Damien the evening before—I shouldn't have answered. I wasn't yet ready to dissect things between us. Shaylia's call had come through while I'd been on the phone with him, exciting me more than hearing Damien's voice. I hung up on him and found myself baffled at the lack of regret. Yes, I missed him, but Shaylia...

She twisted my insides but in the best way. Seeing her smiling face every morning at work the previous two weeks, hearing her soothing, sexy voice, the briefest touch of fingers earlier the day before when she'd handed me a folder... It seemed like a high school crush all over again, butterflies and all, the sexual tension between us almost palpable.

Stolen glances in the office, smiles, and text messages almost every night revealed the obvious, and I wondered about her thoughts toward me. The emotions emanating off her came soft and gentle, overflowing with happiness every time our eyes met. Pupils dominated the blue of her eyes whenever I stared too long, the thrumming pulse beneath the pale skin of her neck salivating my mouth.

Admit it, you're totally smitten with your secretary.

I blew a huge exhale between my lips. I wanted to call her, tell her all about how the gallery had shaped up since she'd been offering her thoughts on the few pieces of furniture I'd shown her online. It had been her idea to go with the muted gray-toned couch rather than the blue I'd considered—because the color reminded me of her eyes.

Falling for her came easy—too easy—but I'd promised a safe work environment, and asking her out, even as a friend, wasn't a good idea.

Heaving another sigh, I considered calling the only other person who might be happy to hear I finally opened a gallery—my mom.

A renowned psychologist with empathic abilities beyond my own, she should have been more sensitive to the little boy starved for her attention—for her love. However, work had always come first, earning her the fame and prestige she longed for. I'd never been number one in her life, something I had accepted years earlier.

She'd sat me down once and told me as empaths, our purpose and value came from helping others. I hated people and their feelings—but she didn't take the time to teach me how to deal with being overwhelmed by both. She'd left me to fend for myself, learning on my own how to deal with the emotions that swamped me on a daily basis.

Throughout my younger years, I'd striven to help those who felt drawn to me, those who spilled their lives to me in a gory, vomitus mess. Crushed beneath their emotions, I failed at fulfilling my purpose as an empath.

I grew up believing I had no value, no use other than being the trash can people tossed their pain into.

Damien was the first person I met who didn't fill my ears with his shit. He'd been the first to show self-control over his emotions—a breath of fresh air. He took me under his wing, once I tossed my trash at him, protecting me when I couldn't do so for myself. I ended up under his hands and body, more often than not, our freshman year.

Heart aching and needing someone to ease my rising pain over the past, I dialed my mom's number. She answered after a few rings.

"Ethan, it's been awhile," she said, sounding preoccupied, same as always when I called.

I made my excuses, then let her speak, half-listening as she filled me in on her busy week of traveling and speaking.

The second she paused, I tossed out my news. "So, I did a thing."

"What thing is that?"

"I rented space to open my own art gallery." I rubbed the microfiber armrest of the couch, needing to get to the point before she made excuses to get off the phone and get back to whatever she'd been doing.

"That's lovely, Ethan."

Her dismissive tone dented my brow, and I pursed my lips, ready to hang up.

"And what does Damien think about your new venture?" she asked, probably only because she realized she at least *needed* to converse briefly.

I pinched the bridge of my nose. My mother couldn't even remember our conversation from the Monday morning Damien had left for London when I'd told her we'd broken up. She had offered her condolences before asking if I needed to talk about it.

"I wouldn't know what Damien thinks, Mom," I said, standing and striding back toward the smaller, office area. "We broke up. Remember?"

"Oh, honey. I'm so sorry." The perfect amount of sympathy laced her words—same as the first time she'd said them two weeks prior—but I didn't feel the sincerity I'm sure she'd hoped to convey. "Do you need to talk about it?"

I withheld my snort and offered her the same answer I'd given her before. "No. I have to go." I needed to get off the phone before I said something I shouldn't.

"Take care, Ethan."

"Yeah, you, too." I hung up and tossed my cell onto the small table. Hands on my hips, I eyed the boxes of paintings. Might as well get to work and finish. Perhaps putting up an "open" sign in the door would make me feel better.

My cell caught my gaze. Perhaps calling Shaylia would be even better.

I stretched my neck side to side, head tipped back, focusing on the white ceiling. Everything about Shaylia pulled at me—I couldn't help myself. I grabbed my cell and shot off a quick text to update her on the gallery's progress along with the picture I'd taken after placing the couch against the wall.

Shaylia: **OMG the couch looks awesome! Did you hang any of your pieces? You must be so excited!**

I couldn't help myself and texted back. **I am, but I'm bummed since I don't have anyone to celebrate with.**

I held my breath, hoping my obvious hint wouldn't offend her.

She took her good old time replying—I hung up the first of my paintings while waiting since pacing would only make me more anxious. The dinging of an incoming text slammed my heart in my chest. My hand shook as I swiped my phone's screen to life.

Shaylia: **Can you call me when you get a chance?**

I dialed immediately, her hello melting my insides like warm butter over toast.

"We could meet for drinks to celebrate if you want," she hurried to say, breathless to the point my dick hardened. "I mean, as friends, of course. I'm not asking you out or anything."

I couldn't help but chuckle while adjusting my dick inside my jeans. "How about dinner? *As friends.*"

"Yes." She didn't hesitate, laughing lightly upon answering.

I studied the slash of red I'd smeared on a canvas the night after Damien and I had broken up, expecting a sense of guilt or sorrow to lance my chest. Nothing of the sort happened, and I breathed a bit easier.

"Can I pick you up?" I asked, "Or is that too date-ish?"

"I would like that." Her softened tone hinted at her pleasure, and I couldn't contain my grin or the swelling of my dick.

"Two hours okay?"

"Sure."

I'd already looked up her address in her file and acted the stalker by checking out the area online, but I echoed the street number and name as though jotting them down.

"See you soon," I murmured and gripped my hard length through my jeans, knowing I needed to ease the ache in my balls before going to pick her up.

I pulled into the driveway of the tiny rental I'd seen on Google Maps, quickly taking in the brown-sided shack with its neatly mowed grass and swarm of white and pink flowers covering the bushes along the foundation. Their sweet perfume filled my lungs as I stepped out of my car, breathing deep to calm my nerves.

I hadn't been as nervous since I'd first met Damien in our dorm room years earlier. The shakes plagued my legs and hands, and sweat dotted my brow even though the day's heat had subsided a bit.

Shaylia pulled open the door as I approached, her face flushed, her blue eyes alight with the happiness I could feel pouring off her.

"Hey." She pulled the door closed, the other hand behind her back, and I stared at the fall of dark hair—she kept pulled up at work—hanging over her shoulders, the swell of her breasts neatly tucked into a tight tank top littered with pale flowers. Skinny jeans hugged her curves and ended at her ankles where strappy sandals encased her feet.

I swallowed back my groan at seeing her in something other than her usual office attire. "You look great," I managed, hating that my face heated.

"Thanks. So do you."

I'd changed my paint-splattered jeans for a darker pair and opted for a dark green polo shirt and loafers. Casual but nice enough to eat at a decent restaurant if that's what she preferred.

"Here."

I glanced down at her outstretched hand she'd pulled from behind her back to find a box of Necco Wafers. Shaylia had remembered my favorite candy. She'd thought of me outside of the office enough to go out of her way to purchase not just a sleeve but an entire box of the wafers.

A slew of emotions, all my own, mixed in my head and heart. My throat thickened as I took the gift from her hands, unsure if I should tell her no one had done such a thoughtful thing for me in as long as I could remember.

"Figured since you didn't have any on your desk the last two days..." Shaylia rubbed her hands down her thighs, and I lifted my focus to her face, my heart thrumming.

"You noticed that, did you?" I managed to get out.

Her smile hit me like a hurricane, stealing my breath and sending a rush of wind through my ears. She shrugged, but her pleasure at *my* pleasure swelled inside me.

Losing my heart would be too damn easy.

I cleared my throat and tucked the box under my arm. "That was very thoughtful. Thank you."

"Sure."

"Ready to go?" I asked since I wasn't sure if I should hug her or kiss her smiling lips like I longed to do.

"Yes."

I motioned her toward the passenger door and opened it for her, shutting her in my Mercedes Cabriolet and thinking I could get used to doing so. The second I settled beside her, the sweet cherry scent of her rolled over me, watering my mouth.

"What are you hungry for?" I asked, rather than tell her she smelled good enough to eat.

"Pizza, burgers, pasta ... whatever you want."

"You don't care?"

She shrugged again, her smile dazzling. "I'm a sucker for pasta."

"I know the perfect place." I put the car in reverse and stole my little secretary away for an evening of wining and dining.

I had no intention of forcing things to progress between us, but I decided as we hit Route 1 South, and the comfort of her warmed me clear through to my bones, I wouldn't turn away the opportunity for more.

Office romance being wrong—so far off the deep end for me—Shaylia's impact on my life, on my happiness couldn't be ignored any longer.

Chapter 6

Shaylia

I didn't take risks, but Ethan's personality enticed me to take the chance of getting to know him better. The fact my position as a temp would be up in four weeks made that decision easier.

While I enjoyed working for Fiorenza Financial alongside Madeline, Ethan was by far a bigger prize. His obvious interest in me blew whatever walls I thought to protect my vulnerability into dust. Sexy as hell and sweet to boot, I didn't understand his bare ring finger on his left hand.

"What?" Ethan asked.

I jerked my attention off his hand, my face heating in the Italian restaurant's dim lighting. We sat in a basement of sorts in a tiny place in the North End, sipping our wine and chatting about his gallery, muted opera cascading in the background. "Hmm?"

"You were staring at my hand." He wiggled his fingers, tapping his index on the cloth-covered table.

"Oh." My laughter felt forced, my voice shaky. "That." I sipped my wine, unable to hold his gaze. "I was, um … wondering why you aren't married."

He didn't respond right away to my spewed words, and I dared to glance up. A heavy sigh escaped his lips. "Kind of a long story."

"I'm all ears."

The waiter arrived with our meals before another word passed between us. I eyed my shrimp scampi and the bed of linguini beneath, my mouth watering. Once the waiter left us, Ethan chuckled.

"Dig in," he said, still laughing. "I'll fill you in while we eat."

I twirled my pasta and tried for a dainty bite, but ended up with a mouthful.

Ethan's smile lingered. "I love that you love food."

"Mmm." I swallowed a few seconds later, my mouth happier than it had been for months. "I *do* love food."

He took a bite of his lasagna, watching as I twirled another forkful of pasta.

We both smiled.

"So the marriage thing," he finally said, glancing down to cut another bite with the edge of his fork. "I've been seeing the same person for fifteen years."

Present tense.

"Fifteen?" I nearly choked on my shrimp and needed to wash it down with a sip of wine.

"Yes, and it recently took a sour turn. When your partner doesn't support your desires, your dreams..." Ethan shrugged and lifted his fork toward his mouth. "I felt like I was drowning, losing myself."

I felt bad for him, but the sudden thought I might be a rebound stole my breath.

"You left her?"

A corner of Ethan's lips lifted as he chewed and swallowed, but not out of amusement. "Him."

"Oh." I blinked, trying to not act surprised—and disappointed. *He's gay ... of course he's gay. He's too sweet, too kind—*

"I'm bi," Ethan said before I could wrap my head around him being gay and our relationship destined to remain friends.

"Oh," I repeated, still fighting for something else to say.

"We met fifteen years ago in college, and we've been together ever since."

"He didn't support your dream of opening the gallery?"

"No." Ethan glanced away, his brow furrowing. "And after all I've done for him..." He shrugged and took another bite.

"I'm not sure I should say I'm sorry it ended," I said, needing to be honest but encouraging. "Especially since you seem so happy with the decision you made to open your gallery."

"I'm not really sorry either." His smile appeared genuine even though pain remained in his eyes when he glanced up at me. He inhaled deeply, his defined chest rising beneath the cotton hugging his pectorals. "It's time for a new beginning."

I quickly wiped my mouth and lifted my wine glass as he held his up.

"To trying something new," he murmured his toast, searching my eyes.

"I'll drink to that," I heard myself reply, my voice low and rasped, my arousal so damn obvious, my cheeks heated. Warmth sprang to life between my thighs, and I couldn't tear my gaze from his. "You can't help who you love," I said after sipping, hoping to ease the sexual tension energizing the air between us, wanting him to know I didn't judge him for his sexuality.

"No, I don't suppose you can." Ethan took a bite of his lasagna, and moments later, launched into the tale of meeting Damien Fiorenza—the owner of the firm we both worked for.

Fiorenza. My heart sank to the bottom of my toes.

I didn't just have the hots for my boss—no. I had the hots for the ex of my boss' boss. Could that fact be any more fucked-up? Deciding it was *good* I would be leaving their firm sooner than later, I listened as Ethan told me a little about their history.

I couldn't imagine his anxiety over the entire situation. He was VP of his ex-partner's firm, still living in the same apartment even though our boss had traveled overseas to open the new office in London.

"What are you going to do?" I asked as Ethan finished spilling his guts, our plates cleaned of every last bite of pasta.

He pursed his lips for a moment, setting his fork upside down atop his plate. "Damien and I obviously need to discuss where to go from here with our condo and the firm," he finally said, sitting back in his chair. "He's been such a big part of my life for so long, I'll admit it will be hard letting go completely and moving on."

Ethan peered at me as I held my silence, unsure if he saw me as a rebound as I feared.

"It's nice to have someone to talk to—to have a friend like you," he murmured, his tone hinting at more—perhaps that was just wishful thinking.

I chewed the inside of my lip for a few seconds, thoughts and emotions tumbling through me.

"What's bothering you?" Ethan asked, his gaze steady —probing. "Your feelings aren't usually this loud."

"Sorry."

"Don't be sorry." He smiled. "You're a breath of fresh air with your subdued emotions."

Screw it. I needed to toss it out, let him know—clear the air and perhaps move on in my head over the entire situation of wanting my boss.

"This feels like a lot more than friends," I whispered, my pulse thrumming, my fingers clenched together in my lap.

Ethan slid his hand over the table, palm up.

I stared a few heartbeats before sliding my fingertips along his. Electrical waves swept up my arm, down through my body, and straight to my suddenly throbbing clit. It had been too long since I'd allowed someone to touch me.

"Can I show you my gallery?" Ethan asked, leaning forward, his gaze imploring.

Unable to find my voice, I nodded.

He hadn't agreed with what I'd made note of, but he also hadn't laughed it off. The fact he held my hand while heading out into the summer night—his long fingers pressing around mine as though our hands ought to be clasped—lightened my heartbeat and my breathing.

We walked the two blocks to his car in silence, the sounds of the Boston night a drone of buzzed nothing in my ears.

His gallery would offer privacy, something we'd had momentarily a few times in the previous two weeks inside his office—before our non-date. What would happen once alone with no chance of interruption? A mere showing of his gallery? More? Would he attempt to kiss me? Did I want him to?

Hell to the yes and then some.

My nerves got the best of me, and I fought not to fidget or shake while he drove us south toward the store front he rented. My mind went wild with what might or might not happen.

I dug into my small purse and pulled out a pack of wild cherry LifeSavers.

"You're nervous." Ethan didn't ask a question, but I found myself nodding as we sat at a red light and I popped a candy into my mouth. "You needn't be," he murmured, glancing over at me, his eyes glinting in a passing car's headlights.

"You always make me nervous," I admitted, managing to hold his gaze.

"Is that a good thing?"

"Yes?" I tossed out, not really sure, my head jerking in a nod.

"I won't make a pass at you," he murmured. "I won't touch you—unless you want me to."

I heaved a heavy breath, wanting to tell him so many contradictory things, my head spun. *Yes, no, maybe? Kiss me senseless, slam me against the wall, and fuck this tension out of my system.*

"Let's just take one moment at a time, see where it leads us, okay?"

I nodded again, crunching on my candy. The devil on my shoulder whispered how much we wanted Ethan's hands and mouth on us while the angel reminded me of my past, of the ex-boss who'd made advances.

And how that situation ended up.

My brow furrowed slightly at the thought, and I popped another candy in my mouth. Nothing I had done or said instigated my ex-boss' attention. I had been nothing but professional, keeping my hands to myself —he hadn't inspired me otherwise—and my mouth shut whenever he'd dropped hints about finding me desirable. The groping hadn't been encouraged by me, thus the lawsuit.

"You're overthinking," Ethan said as he parked his car.

"My thoughts are that loud?"

He chuckled again. "You're chewing that LifeSaver to bits."

I laughed as he hopped out of the car. Since he seemed to enjoy being the gentleman, I waited for him to round the vehicle and open the passenger door for me.

"Thank you."

"My pleasure." His eyes twinkled in the night as he once more gathered my hand.

The way his voice rumbled over the word 'pleasure' rushed moisture to gather between my thighs. I bit back my moan as he unlocked the door flanked by huge glass pane windows, their pulled blinds hiding what lay behind. He flicked on the lights, and I breathed in the lingering fumes of new paint and furniture polish as I stepped into the interior.

He'd strung lights along the ceiling, all but one highlighting the light gray of the bare walls. One painting hung alone—beside the gray couch I'd encouraged him to purchase.

Red, angry slashes crossed the canvas, hints of blue shadows in their wake, a burst of yellow in the background.

"I painted that the night Damien left," Ethan said as I stepped closer to study the abstract painting. "The same day I met you."

Did he see me as the sunlight, the life-bringer, or did the red's outward journey represent his escape from what he thought had given him life for fifteen years?

"It's beautiful," I said, determined to not ask about the emotions that inspired the piece.

"You've been a ray of sunshine kissing my skin ever since you walked into my office."

Oh God. Swallowing, I turned, my heart leaping as Ethan threaded his fingers through mine once more and stepped closer, leaving mere inches between us

"You're scared," he murmured, his focus on my mouth.

"Nervous," I corrected, my tone barely present.

He sucked his lower lip between his teeth without breaking his stare from mine. "Dance with me?"

No music floated in the gallery's still air, but I stepped even closer as he tugged, my breath catching as he settled our clasped hands against his chest, his other one dropping to my waist in a light hold. We swayed in silence, our breath shared, our gazes latched, bodies brushing as we moved. My nipples strained against the lace of my bra. Wetness soaked my panties.

But the non-physical draw, the communion of souls, tempted me more than the thought of sex. I'd never felt connected to another human like Ethan. Yes, he could feel my emotions, and while that truth would probably scare most, I enjoyed the fact. There would be no hiding from Ethan, fewer chances of misunderstandings that often ruined relationships.

"Can I kiss you?" he murmured, his focus dropping to my mouth.

Yes, oh God, yes.

I managed to nod as the devil's moaned words whispered in my head.

The brush of Ethan's soft lips against mine sagged my knees, and I clutched at the back of his shirt as he swept them across and back again, soft and gentle— the same as everything about Ethan.

My heart melted—gone to goo in the blink of an eye.

Ethan's hold on my waist tightened, and he flicked his tongue along the seam of my lips. Moisture rushed to coat my already soaked panties, my pulse thrumming loudly in my ears as we pressed closer, his hard body tight against mine. I parted my lips, and we both moaned as our tongues caressed each other's, tasting and exploring what might be. What *shouldn't* be.

All thought swept away as the vibrating energy between us exploded in an array of colors behind my eyelids. He tasted of sweetness and wine, man and ... *rightness.*

Not *right*, the angel on my shoulder muttered.

I pulled back, heaving for breath. "I want you more than anything, but this isn't a good idea, Ethan," I somehow managed to whisper the truth past my raging libido demanding more, more, *more.* "You're my boss."

Only for a few more weeks.

I clenched my eyes shut tight at the devil's words.

Ethan expelled a heavy sigh and rested his forehead against mine, continuing to hold me close. "I forgot what it's like to feel a woman's softness," he murmured. "It's addictive. *You're* addictive. You taste like the sweetest cherries."

A shaky laugh blew past my lips. "That's the LifeSavers—"

He swooped down, capturing my mouth again with a low groan I felt deep inside me, fluttering the muscles inside my pussy, clenching my walls against the emptiness I wanted filled more than I wanted air. Ethan's hands tangled in my hair, angling my head to deepen our kiss, and I clutched at his shirt to remain upright.

All sense of self, of self-preservation flew right out the damn door at the taste of his breath, the claiming of his persuasive lips—the lean, hard muscle pressing against every inch of my front.

Yes, yes, yes, my devil whispered, the angel falling silent as though she too couldn't resist the pull of Ethan's hungry kiss.

His hold loosened in my hair, and he slid one hand down my back to cup my ass, pulling me tighter against his hard length pressing into my lower belly.

Soaked and panting, I fought squirming against him, fought the need to grind like a horny, too-long celibate woman in need of getting laid.

It was Ethan who pulled away, leaving me wanting, my ears ringing. It was Ethan who murmured something about taking me back home.

Fearing I faced sure heartache, I followed along, more than willing to be led to my doom as he pulled me outside into the night.

Chapter 7

Ethan

My dick ached with need I hadn't felt for years. While I'd enjoyed a woman a time or ten in my past in a threesome with Damien, I'd never been so rock hard for the wet warmth between feminine thighs—Shaylia's thighs.

She got me on a level most didn't, and while I expected that was due to the fact I didn't allow too many people to get close to me, I couldn't deny the attraction between us, the feeling of rightness of having her hand in mine.

I fought to keep to the speed limit while heading north out of the city, my thumb rubbing circles on the back of her hand resting on my thigh. Her lips, the taste of her mouth had obliterated all thought of everyone but her, and it wasn't until I'd pulled away, the image of Damien's face flashed in my mind—but without the guilt I'd expected.

It had been his decision to not support my dreams, and although I'd been the one to break things off with him, I felt he had instigated the situation with his inability to bend.

I still loved him, though. Fuck, did I love him. I missed him and his heavy hand, the way he so easily owned my body. But the softness of the woman beside me brought out another side of myself I'd lost touch with over the years—Ethan, the man who wished to dominate for a change, albeit gently.

Soft music sounded from the car's stereo, filling the sexually charged tense silence between us. I wanted to spill every last thought, share every emotion and fantasy with her because I somehow knew she wouldn't judge me. She wouldn't laugh or scoff at how in tune I'd become with myself.

I pulled into her driveway, my headlights flooding the brown siding and the profusion of flowering bushes. One last squeeze on her hand and I released my hold to put the car into park. Shifting to face her, I attempted to study her face in the lack of light.

"Would you like to come in?" She attempted a smile, her nervousness obvious even though I couldn't see her eyes clearly.

My dick jerked in my jeans, hard since kissing her, leaking enough pre-cum, I'd be embarrassed if we ended up where I dreamed the night might go.

"If you'd like me to," I answered, my voice hoarse from the lust simmering inside me.

Shaylia nodded, and for the first time that night, she opened her door before I could round the car.

"Excuse the mess," she said, stepping over the threshold into a tiny kitchen. A door stood open on the right, revealing an equally small bedroom, the queen-size bed neatly made with tucked corners. The living room was straight ahead, a throw blanket tossed over the worn couch the only evidence of anything out of order.

"Mess?" I chuckled and closed the door behind us as she set her purse on the small table beyond the bedroom door. "I've never seen such a tidy home."

"It isn't much, but it gets the job done." Shaylia pulled open the fridge door, and I filled my eyes full of her round ass as she stood with her back toward me. "Beer? Wine?"

She'd seemed receptive to my advances earlier, like putty in my hands, so I decided to bypass the possible awkwardness and tell her the truth. "I'd rather taste you."

A shudder rippled through her. She shut the fridge door, turning toward me, her eyes wide, her pupils eating up the blue surrounding them. She licked her lower lip, drawing my gaze downward to its plump temptation. Need swirled between us, requiring a mere spark to combust, but I kept from reaching for her.

She hesitated long enough, I questioned what laid between us, but she finally took a step closer, laying her palm against my heart. The heat of her touch seared through my shirt, and for the first time in my life, I wished to not just feel a person's emotions but to *know* them—the thoughts behind them.

"Your heart is pounding," she whispered, her head tipped back to hold my gaze, the shakiness in her voice letting me know hers did the same.

I groaned with the need to kiss her, but being a gentleman came first. "We don't need to take this any further if you don't want to. If you're uncomfortable in any way."

She didn't reply and didn't initiate anything as we studied one another in the silence.

"*I've* never wanted anything more," I admitted when the silence became too much. "But I also don't want you to think I'm only doing this to hurt Damien or to help myself move on."

Shaylia searched my face, a slow smile coaxing her lips upward. "I can't feel your emotions as you do mine, but I believe you, Ethan. There's something between us, something I find intriguing enough, I'm tossing all caution out the window—something I rarely do."

I cradled her head in my hands, lightly brushing my thumb over her smile, so damn full of need to give, to lavish attention, and offer release, I lost my voice.

"You turn me on," she murmured, pressing her curves against me. "I do want this—even if you are my boss."

A rush of adrenaline drove through me as I bent to claim her lips. Her breath caught, and I groaned as she parted her lips, allowing me to taste her, to caress her tongue with my own.

My dick strained in my jeans, and I groaned as she rubbed against me, the whimper in her throat oozing more pre-cum from my slit.

"I want this, too," I murmured against her lips. "I want *you*."

She pulled away, and I let her go, my hands shaking, my mouth drying as she kicked off her sandals and reached for the hem of her tank. "I'll show you mine if you show me yours."

I snorted a laugh, grateful to have the nervous tension released a bit. My kicked-off loafers joined her shoes, and I pulled my shirt off over my head, still grinning like a fool.

"Oh God." Her whisper, her hot gaze sliding down over my torso, flexing my abs, and I grabbed myself through my jeans, my smile quickly fading.

"Your turn," I managed to rasp, squeezing my dick to calm the fuck down.

She pulled her tank top off, her long hair swishing back down to caress the white lace of her bra and the dark nipples straining inside, begging for my teeth. I swallowed a sudden rush of saliva and lifted my gaze to her face. Lips parted, she stared at me.

"Your turn." Her breathless siren tone nearly buckled my knees.

Time to reveal what she did to me—embarrassment be damned, I no longer cared. I shoved down my jeans and boxers, stepping out of them, leaving myself bare for her perusal.

Shaylia swallowed, her attention flitting down over me, her gaze snaring on my throbbing dick. She peeled off her jeans quick as fuck, taking her lace panties with them, leaving *me* gawking and swallowing.

She'd shaved her pussy bare, the swollen lips glistening her arousal, her clit peeking from the top, pink and erect.

She reached behind her to unclasp her bra, but I moved in, encasing her body in my arms and attacking her mouth like a starving animal. My dick ached to bury inside her, take her roughly against the wall. I went so far to lift her up, pressing her there as her legs wound around my waist, the wet heat of her pussy resting against the back of my throbbing dick.

"Fuck." I tipped my forehead against hers, fighting to steady my breath, to hold myself in check.

"Yes, please."

"I hadn't ... planned for this." I huffed another laugh.

"I didn't either," she whispered, "but there's nothing to worry about on my end."

I pulled my head back to look her in the eyes as she wiggled in my arms, smearing wetness along my dick. "Same here."

"Then take me bare, Ethan. Please. I-I need to feel you inside me."

I closed my eyes for a moment—a mere breath—and pulled her away from the wall, my hand clasping the soft curve of her ass. "Not here." A dozen steps took us into her dimly lit bedroom, and I laid her back on her bed, settling atop her.

I kissed her lips, her throat, the tips of her breasts, suckling on her tight nipples. Every whimper, every moan she emitted rushed need through me, but I forced myself to move slowly, every sip of her like a fine wine, a gift to be thoroughly enjoyed before consumption.

Her fingers pulled at my hair as I dipped my tongue into her navel and wrapped my arms around her legs.

"Yes..." Her whisper died away as I reached my destination, my nose sliding over her clit while I breathed in her sweet musk. One long lick filled my senses with her, coated my tongue with her creamy arousal, and forced me to swallow the drool flooding my mouth.

So sweet, so ... *female*. God, how had I lived without a woman for so damn long?

I dove in for another taste, groaning and leaking pre-cum with abandon as she clutched her thighs against my ears. While I didn't have much experience pleasuring a woman with my mouth, she writhed beneath my lapping tongue and the light nips of my teeth. The second I closed my lips over her clit, she gasped and arched.

"Oh." Her gulp and whimper coursed the feeling of being a god through my entire body. She yanked on my hair, and I moved up her torso, kissing the softness of her stomach and breasts. The second our lips touched, she wrapped her legs around me, yanking me close.

I loomed on the edge of a cliff, knowing the leap would change me forever, but I'd never wanted anything so damn bad in my life. A shift of my hips angled the tip of my dick against her wet heat, and I lifted my head to catch her gaze.

"You're sure?" I managed to rasp, barely holding onto my restraint from thrusting like an animal.

"Please," she whispered, digging her heels into my ass.

I flexed beneath her, my entire body tense, tight as fuck, sliding balls-deep into her soaked pussy. She arched beneath me, gasping, and I held still against her womb, fighting the brewing in my balls as we stared at one another, lips parted, our breaths shared.

Emotions swirled like a vortex, consuming all thought as I peered into her eyes and dragged out slowly, the clutch of her inner walls trying to suck me back in. Another flex of my ass slid me inside, seated deep, filling her.

Her cherry-laced, sweet breath wafted over my face as she moaned again, but I held off from kissing her, losing myself to the need to drain my balls dry.

Longing, need...

I could feel both from her, more than matching my own as I kept a slow but steady pace fucking into her. Gazes latched, souls connecting in a way I hadn't expected, in a way I'd never experienced with a woman.

How fast does one fall in love? How fast can a crush become a necessity in one's life?

My heart ached in my chest. The base of my spine tingled. The hairs on my nape stood on end as though literal energy crackled the air around us.

Shaylia clutched at my back, her gaze dropping to my lips as she squeezed her inner walls around my thrusting length. "Kiss me, Ethan."

I gave over to the need to fulfill her wish, to offer whatever she desired without any hesitation. I even whimpered, giving into the need to thrust harder, eat at her mouth, breathing in her exhales, swallowing down every gasp I caused by hitting her womb.

I needed to fucking come.

Grasping her ass cheek beneath me, I lifted her hips, angled my own, and ground my pelvis against her.

"Ethan..." She breathed my name as though a prayer, and she came, her back arching, her pussy clamping down on me.

I groaned and buried my face in her neck as tingles raced through my balls. The first eruption of cum through my dick jerked my entire body against hers. I pulled out and thrust again, spurting deep inside her, giving over to the milking muscles of her pussy.

She clutched at me with her thighs, her hand, and fingernails, and the softness of her beneath me, spinning my head, ringing my goddamn ears.

I took her mouth again, pouring every bit of emotion inside of me into our kiss, wanting to give her everything—every part of me, all my thoughts, my entire life.

Leaping off the cliff into the unknown had fulfilled me in a way I'd never expected, but as our kiss grew languid, our heartbeats slowed, I couldn't help but feel something lacked—and not on her part. A piece of my life's puzzle was missing, and the truth of what it was shifted my world's axis.

Chapter 8

Damien

Warm wetness surrounded my cock—a tongue laving along my length—and I groaned, grasping at the head between my thighs. Expecting Ethan's shorter hair, my morning wood flagged for a brief second upon fisting my hands in long hair.

Adrienne. The bar.

She shoved her tongue into my slit, and I growled, thoughts of Ethan fading enough, I thrust upward, making her engulf my length again with her hot mouth.

"Holy *fuck*," I groaned as she dragged her teeth gently over my sensitive flesh.

"I said just the one night," Adrienne said, after popping off my dick, her husky voice tightening my balls. "But I think I want your cock one last time."

I peeled an eyelid up as she slid off the bed and bent over to rifle through her purse for another condom. For a woman, she had one hell of an ass, but the thought of burying myself balls deep inside her puckered hole brought Ethan to the forefront of my mind. Without the numb of alcohol, like the previous evening, my head ruled my body. Jerking my focus off Adrienne, I climbed off the opposite side of the bed and strode toward the bathroom.

"I have a meeting," I said, the lie sliding off my tongue with ease.

"On a Saturday?" I didn't need to turn to see the disappointment I heard in her voice.

"Can you see yourself out?" I asked, pausing in the bathroom's doorway, thankful my hard-on flagged.

"Was I that bad?" she muttered, a hint of a frown denting her brow. She jerked her attention off me to grab up her clothes, re-clasping the bra I'd all but ripped off her the night before.

"You were hot as fuck," I said, needing to ease my guilt at all but kicking her out. "But we agreed to just the one night."

Lips pursed, she set about pulling her clothes on and ran her hands through her hair, attempting to tame what I'd wreaked havoc on.

"Thank you for last night," I forced myself to say, already feeling enough like an asshole because I didn't even *want* to offer her thanks.

"Mmm." Adrienne didn't look at me but grabbed up her purse. "Goodbye, Damien," she murmured without a glance my way and slipped into the hallway, the door clicking shut heavily behind her, leaving me alone.

"Fuck." I pinched the bridge of my nose and breathed deeply a few times, hating myself on so many goddamn levels, I wanted another drink.

I wanted Ethan, missed him so damn much, my chest ached.

I strode across the room, slid the deadbolt, and went straight to the shower where a glob of conditioner helped me ease my morning wood thoughts of Ethan had brought back from the grave. I groaned his name with the first spurt of spunk into my fist, but easing the guilt eating at my gut over Adrienne didn't come as easily.

The attempted phone call the night before hadn't ended well, but I needed to try again. I needed to hear his voice even if only for a moment. He didn't answer. I left for the office, wishing for a double-shot of vodka rather than the coffee my body needed.

Hours later, I returned to my room, drained, my head aching. I longed for Ethan's soothing touch, his ability to know what I needed and when. Rubbing my chest against the ache inside, I hit his speed dial. Same as earlier that morning, he didn't answer. Scowling, I tossed the phone onto the bed. A long, hot shower only slightly revived me, and I picked back up my cell before drying off fully. He hadn't returned my attempted call—again.

I pressed the button to recall him, and it went straight to voice mail.

"Fuck." My stomach an empty pit and grumbling like hell, I decided to head downstairs to eat rather than sit alone and dine on room service. Besides, I needed more than the mere nips in the room's small fridge.

Three vodkas in and one fry-up later, my mood lightened, and I found myself shooting the shit with the bartender, trying and failing like fuck to ignore the woman on the stool beside me.

She smelled like apples and cinnamon, and the curve of her muscular calf above her heels had me thinking all kinds of good thoughts. However, unlike the previous night where I'd only wanted Adrienne, Ethan resided in my thoughts, and my dick ached to have a woman between us again.

I slid off my stool without acknowledging the woman and staggered from the restaurant before my dick got me into trouble again.

Ethan hadn't tried to call me back, but rather than grumble, I booted up my laptop. He'd said we would talk when I got back home, but I needed to get all the thoughts out of my buzzed head and send them immediately.

Halfway to drunk and thinking with my emotions and body, I poured my heart and soul into every typed word, telling him how much I needed him ... how much he meant to me ... how much of an ass I'd been over the years, seeming to always take and never give.

I told him I wanted to lavish him with gifts, praised him for being the most perfect partner a man could wish for. I longed to kneel before him as he so did often to me and wrap my arms around his waist to hug him tight, to kiss his feet, giving him the worship he deserved.

Ethan was the love of my fucking life, and I'd gotten too damn caught up with righting my family name and my grandfather's business to give him the time and attention he deserved.

I'd been an asshole for so damn long, and fear over losing him forever because of my mistakes churned my stomach.

Guilt over the whole Adrienne affair tempted me to spill that shit, too, but I withheld. That sort of confession came best in person, and in the back of my mind, I half-hoped, I would forget the affair ever happened before telling the truth became necessary. Admitting to sleeping with someone other than him—even if we *had* broken up—would tear us apart completely before I had a chance to make amends.

I re-read my lengthy apology, fixing a word here and there to better fit what I meant to say since intonation and voice inflections lost themselves in cyberspace communications. One heavy exhale, and I hit send, realizing too late I'd sent it to his work email address, which he wouldn't check until Monday morning.

While I wanted to change my flight home and talk to Ethan the second he finished reading my email, I thought of the man I would leave in charge of the London office, and how ready he might be to stand on his own for a short time. The truth was, he wasn't.

There wouldn't be an earlier than planned escape from London for me. It would be up to my email and hopefully, a resulting phone call to make things right, but I felt my words would at least be the opening I needed to make amends.

My mood somewhat lightened and feeling a bit more hopeful, I shut down my computer and crawled into the empty bed, thoughts of how I could show Ethan my love and support taking over my mind until the vodka and sleep claimed me.

Chapter 9

Shaylia

Tearing my focus off Ethan's parted lips as he slept physically hurt, but I shifted away from the heat of his body beside mine and slipped out of bed. The sun hadn't yet fully risen, but my bladder and the idea of coffee urged me to move—even if thoughts of making love to him again attempted to persuade me otherwise.

We hadn't stopped touching, kissing, or talking until late into the night when he rolled me over and settled between my thighs for a second time. It hadn't been fucking. What I had with Ethan went far beyond what I'd ever experienced before.

The connection between us, looking into one another's eyes while he filled me had me thinking of making love rather than fucking. It had been intense—an emotional upheaval, yet satisfying on a deeper level than I'd ever known.

I glanced at him once more, his dark hair mussed, hand shoved beneath the pillow he rested his head on.

My pillow in my bed.

Happiness bubbled inside me, making me want to crawl right back under those covers with him again.

Bladder before you make a puddle on the floor.

I pulled on a long t-shirt and panties before leaving Ethan behind, gently closing the door behind me. Expelling a long breath, I made my way to the bathroom to take care of business before readying the coffee pot.

I found myself humming while pulling down two mugs, and my smile widened. He admitted to having a love affair with French toast, so I pulled a loaf of bread from the freezer, strangely elated about making him breakfast.

The last man I'd wanted to spoil in such a way had been my father. I refused to let the broken heart he'd left behind hinder what Ethan and I might have found. It had been years since I'd seen my father, years since he'd torn our family apart, but the hurt of a little girl still festered. Insecurity over never being enough lingered, feeding fuel to the fire within me for perfection, to be the best I could be—for myself and those around me.

Unfortunately, the temptation to never trust again remained all-too real as well, but Ethan...

I sighed.

He seemed so genuine, our connection so deep, I couldn't help but give him the benefit of the doubt. Doing so had me giddy as a high schooler crushing, and I wondered if it was possible to fall in love in so short a time.

The bedroom door clicked behind me, and I glanced over my shoulder, my breath catching. Ethan stood in the doorway, boxers low on his hips, revealing the muscled V at his waist and the too-obvious erection tenting the front.

I clenched my thighs together, roaming my focus upward over rock-hard abs and pecs I'd made myself well-acquainted with and the trimmed beard that had reddened the skin between my thighs and on my neck the night before. Green eyes, not fully awake, peered at me and combined with his slow smile, made a mess of the new panties I'd pulled on moments earlier.

"You're so damn sexy in the morning," I said, my heartbeat picking up pace.

"So are you." He started toward me, his gaze flicking down over my bare legs before backing me against the counter, his arms winding around my waist. "Morning."

"Good morning to you." I smiled, wanting to drown in his sleepy eyes.

The coffee pot gurgled the last of the water atop the grinds as Ethan lifted me up onto the counter beside it. Stepping close between my spread thighs, he yanked me to the counter's edge.

"I want you again," he said, tilting his forehead against mine.

"I can tell," I said, biting back giddy laughter as he thrust against the soaked cotton of my panties. I ran my fingers through his hair and pulled his head back so I could see his face. "I want you, too."

Ethan groaned and shoved down his boxers enough to free his straining length. Same as the night before, sexy as hell pre-cum oozed from the tip. He jerked himself slowly, his gaze dropping to my panties.

I thought to hop down and shimmy out of them, but he slipped a finger along the edge, tugging them to the side and pressed the head of his cock against my opening with the other hand.

"Look at me."

My head jerked up to meet his gaze as he slowly pressed into me. I held tight to his hair, moaning as he filled me, stretched me to capacity.

"I think I found heaven," he murmured with a smile while his balls rested against my body.

I squeezed my inner walls around him, and he groaned.

"The noises you make..." I whispered. "They melt me even more than your words."

He lifted me into his arms and took my mouth, all thoughts of morning breath or my being too heavy flitting away on the feeling of being fully seated on his cock and the strength of his arms as he lifted and lowered me, over and over. I squirmed, whimpered my need for more, but he held to his slow, relentless pace, driving me bat-shit crazy. Sweat slicked his shoulders, but still, he fucked into me, unhurried yet relentless, standing right there in my kitchen.

"Please, Ethan," I begged, my entire body shaking along with my voice.

He lifted me off him without a word and set me on my feet, spinning me toward the counter. I leaned forward with gratitude, the countertop cool against my cheek as he kicked my legs wide—and ripped my panties off with one yank.

"Hold on, baby."

Ethan filled me with one thrust, and I gasped, lifting my ass toward him, every inch of my skin tingling, thrilled with his show of aggression, something I hadn't gotten a glimpse of the night before.

As though he'd woken fully, he plowed into me, over and over, his arm banded around my waist, keeping me from bruising myself against the counter's edge. The heat of him covered my back, his beard scraping my neck with every drive of his hips.

My legs lost their strength, but he held me up, his other hand sliding down over my pubis to where he thrust into me.

"You feel like heaven, Shaylia," he murmured against my neck, his fingertips sliding up to find my clit. "I need you to come around me. Clench down on me like you did last night. Milk my dick dry."

I shuddered at his rumbled words, and the mere flick of his fingertips over my clit sent me soaring. I might have shrieked his name, might have begged him to fuck me harder, deeper. Zero shame over my wanton behavior bothered me—Ethan overrode every sense.

"Fuck," he growled and slammed into me one last time, his cock jerking his own release, filling me with heat and cum.

My ears rang, and my fingertips tingled as he eventually relaxed against me, both of us sweaty and breathless. I didn't want to move, didn't want him to pull out and leave me empty and aching for more.

"Sorry," he murmured on a sigh.

"Mmm." I smiled, my eyes still closed. "For what?"

"For taking you before you had the coffee you live for. For ruining your pink panties."

I laughed, and he grabbed a paper towel from the holder beside me.

"Here." He pulled out and pressed the towel between my thighs to stop the flow of our combined cum.

"You can ruin every pair I have if it releases that animal inside you," I said, my voice sounding all dreamy-like even to my own ears.

Pink stained Ethan's cheeks when I turned fully to find him pulling his boxers back up.

"I had the thought of bending you over like that and couldn't help myself."

Since he seemed more the beta type, I wondered if Damien had ever allowed him control. It was on the tip of my tongue to ask, but I bit down to keep my questions inside. The last thing I wanted was to bring up his ex or possible guilt over sleeping with me.

Ethan eyed the coffee pot.

"Want to shower with me first?" I asked, suddenly feeling shy once more, needing the feel of his arms to tell me I hadn't been dreaming the previous twenty-four hours.

His slow smirk, the softness in his eyes re-melted my heart, one I knew I'd lost to him in a matter of two weeks.

I'd slept with my boss, and I'd like it.

I wanted to do it again, damn the consequences. Ethan had gotten beneath my skin, inside my head and body, and I knew I would never get enough of him.

We made love again, slow and easy in the confines of my tiny shower, and the feels he managed to raise inside me hazed my eyes with tears. Drinking coffee together afterward while snuggled on the couch only heightened my buoyant mood and filled my heart further. I pressed against his side, our fingers twined as birds tweeted outside the open window behind us.

"Would you come to the gallery with me this morning?" Ethan asked. "Help me hang the rest of my artwork?"

"Seriously?" I pulled away, my heart thumping.

"You've been such a help to me already—and while I don't want to take advantage—I enjoy you. Being with you."

Tears stung my eyes.

"I didn't expect to feel this way so quickly," he murmured, squeezing my fingers and peering into my eyes. "But you're a special woman, Shaylia. I can't get you out of my head. I don't want to."

I swallowed against the thickness clogging my throat and nodded. "I would love to," I whispered.

He smiled and kissed me gently. "You make me feel special," he murmured against my lips. "I-I've never had that with anyone."

"No one?" I asked, settling against his side once more.

"Not even my own mother."

I couldn't feel his pain, but his tone said enough. He'd told me while snuggled in bed about her awards, her fame, but he hadn't mentioned anything about their relationship.

Ethan studied our clasped hands, and I waited, giving him time to figure out if he wanted to talk about it or not.

"For an empath, she had no clue about how her life affected me," he eventually said. "Or if she did, she didn't care."

"I'm sorry," I murmured, closing my eyes at the hurt in his voice.

"Damien was the first person whose emotions didn't overwhelm me. He was the first one to accept me without judgement, to wonder how *I* felt about feeling everyone around me."

My heart squeezed at the mention of his ex and the longing in his words. I didn't doubt he still loved Damien, and I fought off the thoughts I might come in second place once our boss returned home.

"He took me under his wing, so to speak, looked out for me, protecting me when I became overwhelmed by crowds." Ethan let out a heavy sigh, and I held my breath, waiting. He set his coffee aside and pulled me into his arms, the slow beat of his heart against my ear soothing. "I'm upsetting you."

I didn't bother lying, but let out a heavy exhale of my own. "My father left us for another woman and her son when I was eight."

"I'm sorry," he murmured against my hair.

My eyes stung again. "It's why I strive to be better, to be enough, so I never come in second place again."

Ethan kissed my head and squeezed me tighter. "But I'm also falling for you, Shaylia, harder and faster than I expected."

"I-I'm not asking you for anything, Ethan. That's not why I told you about my father."

"I know you're not, but not knowing the outcome of what's growing between us unsettles you."

"It does," I admitted.

"Tell you what,"—Ethan stood and pulled me to my feet, wrapping his arms around my waist—"how about we hang out the rest of today, enjoy the hell out of one another, and be open to seeing where this might go?" His soft smile eased my tension. "Because I sure as hell wonder where we're heading."

"So do I."

"Don't strive," Ethan said, "or try to hide your feelings or be perfect. Be you, Shaylia. I'm sold on the fact you're pretty awesome, just the way you are."

Although his words warmed me, I wondered who *I* was. In my quest for perfection, I'd always looked to those I felt stood above me and tried to emulate their lives. I took on the interests of those around me in the hopes of being good enough for them.

Perhaps Ethan knew something about me I wasn't yet aware of. Whatever it was, I hoped—with all my heart—it would keep me from coming in second place.

Chapter 10

Ethan

I'd slept in my own bed Sunday night, and on my way to work Monday morning, I wished I hadn't made that decision. Spending the entire day with Shaylia had been the balm I needed, her happiness overflowing and encouraging my own.

Even the subtle unease she fought to keep to herself didn't affect our time together.

We'd hung every piece of my artwork on the walls and arranged the pieces the local artists I'd contracted had dropped off before heading to the backroom where I showed her how I preferred to paint.

I ended up painting swirls across her stomach, down her creamy thighs, and over the swell of her breasts before sinking deep inside her body. Warm and wet, she'd welcomed me with a sigh, smearing paint and eventually, sweat between us.

My dick swelled, and I adjusted myself, pulling into the parking garage near the firm. Shaylia brought out a part of me I hadn't known existed, one I'd never thought to explore before because Damien always topped me.

Bending her over her counter had been the hottest thing I'd ever done, and I'd lost myself to the need to fuck into her willing body. In the end though, when I'd finally given into the ache in my balls, it had been Damien's face flashing behind my clenched eyelids.

I shook my head and climbed from my car, scowling.

While Damien and I had broken up and Shaylia and I didn't have an actual understanding, I felt like a lying, cheating bastard.

The sight of her behind her desk, cheeks pink, her blue eyes filled with insecurity hit me like a two-ton bag of bricks, stealing my breath and making me hard as fuck, regardless of the guilt. I bid her and Madeline a good morning but requested Shaylia follow me into my office.

Once shut in, I dropped my bag and yanked her against me, taking her mouth in a bruising kiss.

"I missed you last night," I said, nuzzling beneath her ear, breathing in the scent of cherries.

"You should have stayed with me," she said with a sigh, her entire body pliant in my arms.

"Yes." I'd said no the night before and couldn't for the life of me figure out why. Her softness surrounded me, her happiness soothing, easing my annoyance with having to come into the office at all.

"If you keep kissing my neck like that," she whispered with a giggle, "you're going to leave a nice red rash for everyone to see."

"I'd rather bend you over my desk and fuck the strength right out of your legs."

"God," she whispered, shuddering in my arms. "I wouldn't be able to keep quiet, and I don't think Madeline would appreciate hearing me telling you to fuck me harder."

"Damnit." I pulled away with an exaggerated sigh but didn't loosen my hold on her waist while checking out her sundress. "You look good in red."

"Thanks." Her blue eyes sparkled, shining the joy I could feel coming off her in waves.

"You make me very happy, Shaylia."

She blinked, her smile fading although her happiness didn't. "This is hardly proper for boss and employee."

"Well, screw everyone who thinks that," I said with a fake scowl. "In two weeks, I'm dropping my hours to part-time, and if the gallery does well, I don't plan on *being* your boss any longer."

"I would hate not seeing you every day." Shaylia wound her arms around my neck and pressed her soft breasts against me.

"Who says you wouldn't?"

My phone rang, and I dropped one last lingering kiss on her bare lips before tearing my hands from her curves. I patted her ass as she turned away, hard enough to earn a squeak and flush her face as she glanced over her shoulder at me. I raised an eyebrow as if to ask if she liked it, and her face reddened even more before she turned and scurried away.

My heart light, my grin wide, I grabbed my bag and headed toward my desk, the desk I'd told her I wanted to bend her over—just as Damien had done to me countless times while staying after hours.

The ringing of my phone cut off before I could get a handle on myself.

"Fuck." I slumped down in my chair and booted up my computer, fighting a losing battle over focusing on the next eight hours.

With Shaylia so close, within reach, my dick hard and needy, perhaps taking her where Damien had held me down would erase some of the old memories and give me new. I glanced at his closed office door, hating that my chest ached to see it pull open, his dark gaze eye-fucking me.

My dick jerked in my slacks, going full-on hard again.

I clenched my eyes shut and talked myself down, fighting like fuck to *focus*.

An email from Damien in my inbox snagged my attention the second I opened my eyes, but I stared at the subject line, "I'm sorry" a few long moments before clicking it open.

I'd always thought it was a good thing I could feel Damien's emotions since he wasn't so great at expressing them outside of anger. The words he'd written—vodka induced, I felt sure—ran on and on, but the ramblings of apology, praise, and edification, rather than spewing out what *he* wanted for a change, left me slack-jawed, my heart beating heavy in my chest.

He'd written I deserved more. I deserved a loving partner who appreciated me, one who would put me first in all things. He was proud of the steps I'd taken toward my lifetime dream, and the one time he mentioned what he wanted was hoping he would have the opportunity to support me in the future.

I've loved you for almost half my life, and even though I've made a mess of what we've shared, I'm hoping to make it up to you when I come home.

My throat thickened as longing for him rolled over me, leaving me empty as I re-read his final line a second time.

Shaylia's words from Saturday night, saying we couldn't help who we loved, echoed in my head—but what if I loved *two* people?

I imagined a life without Damien and couldn't fathom one—I couldn't remember my life without him. I imagined going back with him, to the changed man he claimed he wanted to be for me, but the thought of losing Shaylia sat like a rock in my stomach.

"What a fucking mess." I pursed my lips, wondering what the hell I should do, torn, hurting, and lusting, all at once.

My past, my love for Damien was real, but so were my growing feelings for Shaylia. She pushed me to grow, supported me in ways even my mother didn't, in ways Damien hadn't either.

But could Damien change back to the man he'd been before his world had turned upside down in college? Had losing me made him realize how special a relationship we had, how much better it could be?

Fuck.

The curse echoed in my head but not out of need to come with overwhelming force as Shaylia inspired.

I'd been so full all weekend, riding a high of shared emotions with her, but one email left me floundering, wondering what I needed to do to find true happiness.

Chapter 11

Shaylia

For how well my Monday morning started off, it went stale pretty damn quickly. Ethan stayed shut up in his office and only ventured out briefly in the afternoon. His lack of eye contact and thinned lips played with my head, which I fought to keep locked up so as not to upset him.

Did he put on an act to keep the office in the dark about our affair, or did he truly change his thoughts about me within a few hours?

Unable to help myself, I spent the day overthinking, chewing a thumbnail to death before five when he buzzed Madeline over the intercom to let her know he was staying late. My heart leapt—and fell a second later when he told us both over the speaker to take off for the day.

Swallowing back tears, I left the office, my steps heavy, my heart even more so. I didn't text or call him that night, and he didn't reach out to me either.

Thoughts I'd been used slammed my insecurities back firmly into place. All excitement I'd felt over possibly being enough faded with every passing minute. I had allowed myself to hope, only to be played again. While my threatening tears didn't compare to what my father had caused, I still hurt.

Half sick to my stomach, I skipped dinner and went straight to the wine.

The rising sun earned a groaned from me, but I crawled from bed, bleary-eyed and hungover from my stupid choice to try numbing the pain of Ethan's rejection with a bottle of white.

While showering, I tried telling myself I didn't know what had happened. Perhaps Ethan had gotten bad news at work. Perhaps his withdrawal came from something gallery-related. Nothing I imagined helped, however, and by the time I got into work, my stomach threatened to spew the coffee and toast I'd forced down.

The only chance I had to speak with Ethan came while Madeline went to lunch. He exited his office, glanced my way but immediately averted his gaze.

"Ethan?" I called quietly to him as he moved past my desk.

He pulled up short but wouldn't look at me even though no one stood within close proximity.

"Are you okay?" I asked rather than attack or question his silence after spending the weekend in my bed.

He closed his eyes and sighed. "He emailed me."

"Damien?"

"Yes."

I chewed the inside of my lip, my head and heart warring over my own hurt and fears and how Ethan must be feeling. "Are you okay?" I asked again, trying to keep my emotions in check.

"I-I don't know, Shaylia." Ethan glanced around as though to check we were alone, and when his gaze finally landed on me, hurt filled his eyes—for himself or what he planned to do concerning me, I couldn't tell.

I stilled even though my heart slammed in my chest. "Are you going to try working things out with him?" I managed to whisper.

"He wants to."

"Do you?"

"We've been together for so long, it's hard to let go of all the memories, all the emotions."

I didn't understand, but I nodded as he held my gaze.

"You're upset," he said, keeping his voice low.

My attempted smile wobbled and knowing my voice would as well, I shrugged rather than reply.

"I'm upset too."

I couldn't feel his emotions, but reading them on his face made my heart ache even more. "I want you to be happy, Ethan," I somehow blurted without bawling.

Madeline walked around the corner, and I clamped my mouth shut from saying anything else. Grabbing the closest file on my desk, I tore my focus off Ethan.

"I'll get this to you soon," I said, fighting like hell to keep my voice steady.

"Thank you," he replied for Madeline's sake, but I knew he meant it for me as well—for being his friend, for listening and caring, for making him feel special.

Ethan walked off, leaving me with a head full of doubts and a heart torn by insecurity and fear he would go back to the only love he'd known—one so deeply entrenched in his life, I could tell he wasn't ready to move on.

That night, I chewed off my other thumb nail while warring over texting him. I broke down around nine, after two glasses of wine.

Me: **How are you?**

Ethan: **Torn**

Me: **What can I do to help?**

I hoped for a "come over" along with a winking emoji, but neither came through.

Ethan: **Be my friend**

Swallowing back even more tears over what I knew he'd meant, I typed the only thing I could.

Me: If that's what you need, I'll gladly do so.

I tossed my phone aside and threw an arm over my eyes, lounging on my threadbare couch. He just wanted to be friends—the only answer I needed to put to rest the questions in my head. With a huff, I got up to top my glass off.

I woke hungover again, sick to my stomach, head pounding. Temptation to call in sick had me staring at my cell, but I didn't cave. Even though I worked for a temp agency, not giving one hundred percent, being a half-assed employee wasn't part of my strive-for-perfection goal.

Going into work sucked, but I did it with my head held high, a fake smile on my face. I did my job with the skills of an anal retentive organizer—scheduling, filing, shredding, and making calls when needed—in order to dot every 'i' and cross every 't.'

The one time I saw Ethan between his meetings, my smile came easy, actually coaxing one from him. When he seemed so lost, so overwhelmed, my heart ached more for him than myself.

I had promised to be his friend, and if that meant letting him go in hopes he found happiness, I would willingly lay aside my selfish desires.

Chapter 12

Damien

It took Ethan two days to get back to me—two days of agonized waiting and wondering about his frame of mind. I decided if he didn't call or email back before Thursday morning, I would attempt to call him again.

Late Wednesday night—afternoon for him in Boston—my inbox dinged.

My heart seized, seeing the RE alongside his name, and my hand shook while touching the screen to open his email.

He missed me.

I exhaled long and loud before devouring the rest of his written thoughts, wishing I could hear his voice, watch his face as he explained what went on inside his head. How torn he felt over our shared past and moving forward with his dream. Sure they couldn't co-exist, he feared falling back into our old routine, something he refused to do.

Without a promise of changed ways, without my proving myself to him, I knew any chances for a shared future lay closer to zero. I considered writing back, making all the promises in the world, but I hesitated. He couldn't feel my emotions online, wouldn't understand my desire to prove myself unless I stood in front of him, face to face.

Ethan got me. He understood me even when I couldn't find the fucking words to express myself. I wouldn't let him go. I would fight the world to keep him by my side.

Doing so meant packing my shit and heading to the airport, willing to pay whatever fee needed to get me home, willing to leave behind a new office without a solid foundation. I would fall to my knees and beg Ethan for a chance to prove myself, for him to feel everything inside me and know how much I needed him—loved him.

It took too fucking long, but I finally booked a flight back across the pond with a couple stops along the way. Set to arrive in Boston around noon on Thursday and not wanting to wait any longer than necessary, I had no option but to see him in the office and spill my guts.

Chapter 13

Ethan

I walked into work, unable to decide if I was happy or hurt Damien hadn't written back, hadn't called, or texted. I'd laid out my feelings as best I could, as best as mere words allowed, and his lack of communication made me wonder if he'd taken my hesitation as a complete negative when I'd just been trying to lay out my fears before replying, so he would understand where I came from.

Even though I'd taken two days to reply to him, I hated he didn't try calling me, didn't reach out to me in any form whatsoever. I'd done worse by not replying to his reaching out with his email, but it still stung.

When Shaylia came into my office around ten, reserved with her smile and calm in her emotions—and sexy as hell in her tight skirt and heels—I wanted to cry. She was everything a man could hope for—so giving and thoughtful, a great listener, one who put others first.

We only spoke about business, but I stood to see her out, my need to touch her like a ravenous hunger of a man long starved. A mere touch to her elbow zinged electrical charges through me, and she paused to stare into my eyes.

"Ethan."

I closed my eyes at the prayer-like whisper. "I miss you," I muttered, half-choking with my own misery. "I miss *us*."

Her sadness swarmed over me, and tears hazed her eyes when I opened mine. On instinct, I cradled her face in my hands and kissed her with all the tenderness, heart-felt appreciation for her coursing through me.

"Have dinner with me tonight," I begged, pulling back but still holding her face.

"Okay." Her smile eased my aching chest.

My world settled a bit, and I stepped back fully, feeling happier than I had for days as Shaylia scurried out of my office, her cheeks a delicious shade of pink.

* * *

Phone calls for business transactions sucked—especially when if I had a clue about a customer's emotions would help me close the deal. Mr. Roberts droned in my ear as though I gave a shit about his sick hamster, but being an empath, I often heard stories I had no wish to—and I didn't know how to walk away. Damien knew how to pull me from those who drowned me with their emotions...

Eyes closed, I swallowed back my heartache and waited for Mr. Roberts to pause for breath.

"So, what are your thoughts on the plan I emailed over to you last week?" I asked the second it wouldn't sound rude for me to interrupt.

"Oh. Oh, yes, I believe it looks good—all but perhaps that final investment," he said. "I'm too old a codger to consider that new-fangled social media kids can't seem to live without these days."

I could have spun my chair from facing the window overlooking Boston to grab his file, but I knew the updated financial plan I'd put together in Damien's absence for one of our oldest customers.

"I can either remove it completely or offer another option."

He muttered under his breath, something he usually did when on the line. "I suppose you can leave it. I do need to catch up with the times, wouldn't you say?"

"I'll implement the plan immediately, sir." I smiled and agreed.

A door clicked open without a knock, and my dick stirred at the thought Shaylia might have snuck into my office. I attempted to make a goodbye with Mr. Roberts, but the waft of aftershave—woods and musk— sped my heartbeat.

Damien.

"I must go, Mr. Roberts." Hardly more than a ragged whisper, my voice betrayed my sudden anxiety and arousal. I turned, my focus ensnared as Damien drew closer.

Rumpled button-down and slacks more than did his tall, muscular frame justice. A full scruff lined his jaw, and dark piercing eyes peered intently at my face, erasing all but his presence from my mind. My dick stiffened in seconds, and my hand shook as I hung up the phone.

"What are you doing here?" I managed to toss out past my tight throat and chest.

"I needed to talk to you face to face," he said, his focus dropping to my lips as I stood on trembling legs. "You'll believe me if I say what I need to in person."

A shudder rippled through me as Damien entered my personal space—the only man I didn't mind doing so.

"I'll do whatever it takes, Ethan." His dark eyes seared through me, the truth of his words, his determination overtaking my mind. "I'll be receptive to all you say, all you require to be happy because I've realized without you by my side, in my life, it isn't worth living."

My shoulders wilted, the tension of anxiety leaking out of me, but I wasn't about to give in too easily. "My gallery?" I whispered.

"I'll support you in whatever way you need to be happy."

I swallowed, my mouth suddenly dry as dust. "Dropping my hours here to part time?"

A muscle ticked in Damien's jaw, but he nodded. "If that's what you want."

"It is."

"Okay."

I tipped my chin up in an act of defiance that usually brought out his dominant side. "You're not going to have complete control over me anymore, Damien."

"I hate to think I ever made you feel that way." His low tone, his feelings of pain and regret hazed my eyesight.

"I need to be a priority." My voice broke. "Not a side-kick, not a plaything of convenience, not the ace up your sleeve."

His gaze softened to tenderness, and I bit back a moan of need as my dick strained for him. "I'm so sorry, Ethan." His voice ragged, he cupped my cheek, the warmth of his palm penetrating to the deepest parts of me.

My eyelids fluttered closed as I soaked in his apology, the love pouring off him in waves.

"So fucking sorry," he murmured again. "I've been a complete ass for so long, and I don't deserve your forgiveness, but I'm begging for it. Please."

Every inch of me burned for him, every muscle trembling with need. "Kiss me. *Show* me you mean what I'm feeling from you."

Damien closed the distance between our bodies and gave me what I asked for, claiming my mouth with an eagerness I matched. There was no point in fighting for dominance—Damien would always hold that position between us, and I wouldn't have it any other way.

He ground his hard length against mine, the scratch of material, the buffer of clothing between us driving me mad.

"I missed you so fucking much, Ethan," Damien growled against my mouth before nipping my lower lip, his hands clasping my head to hold me still. "I've been so fucking hard for you."

I grabbed his dick and squeezed with the pressure he loved best, a grip verging on pain. "Love you," I managed before he shoved his tongue between my lips, fucking my mouth as I knew he wanted to do to my body.

Damien pulled away, breathless, his dark eyes searching mine even though the magnetism between us spun out of control like always when in close proximity. "What can I do to make it up to you?"

All kinds of thoughts flitted through my head—the desk beside us, asking for permission to top him—but what I wanted most, as always, was to please him.

"You know what I want," I said, yanking on his belt.

He dropped his hold on my face and moved back another few inches, giving me room to free his dick. "You're too fucking good to me, Ethan."

"I can't help but love you," I answered, dropping to my knees.

Chapter 14

Shaylia

I returned from lunch, and Madeline went off with a wave of her fingers. I chewed on the inside of my lip a full minute before deciding to make a move.

Ethan seemed so much better that morning, his mind free, and with his having kissed me and asking me to dinner, I wasn't about to let a moment of possibility pass me by.

I hurried to the bathroom to freshen up, my pulse thrumming, my insides giddy even though the angel on my shoulder begged for caution. Ethan had broken my heart so easily and mended it almost as quickly. Not being hesitant was foolish, but the connection we had, the absolute feeling of being caught up while in his arms proved a strong force for my self-control.

Cheeks flushed and eyes sparkling, I smiled at myself in the mirror before taking a deep breath and making my way back to my desk. Knowing I had at least twenty minutes before Madeline returned, I approached Ethan's office door, unsure if I should knock or just sneak in.

My heart thumped in my chest, the rush of adrenaline spiking in my blood, making my hand shake as I lifted it. My soft knock escaped my own ears with the heartbeat pounding between them, and I leaned toward the door, realizing I might not hear his bid to enter.

"Come in," a low voice barely registered.

I inhaled in an attempt to still my nerves and eased the door open, slipping inside, only to pull up short, blinking at the vision before me.

Ethan knelt on his office floor, his mouth around another man's cock. They peered at one another, completely wrapped up in a world of their own.

My breath caught and my heart stalled before picking up speed as Ethan worked him over, both men moaning their pleasure, unaware their audience of one gawked.

I couldn't look away, couldn't tear my gaze off how beautiful Ethan looked, worshiping who had to be Damien.

And Damien…

Sexy as sin—his head tipped back, his eyes closing as he held Ethan's face in his large hands, fucking into his throat, veins popping in his exposed neck.

"Coming," he growled, and my thighs pressed together at the roughness coating the word—the same word I'd *misheard* through the door.

"Fuck." Damien groaned deep and long, holding Ethan's face close to his groin.

Ethan whimpered, and I glanced down to find he held himself in hand, shots of cum roping across the floor between his knees and Damien's shoes.

Both men shuddered and backed off as one, not tearing their gazes from one another, their lips parted by heaving breaths, heightening my arousal.

A smear of white lay on the corner of Ethan's lips as he peered up at Damien with love and adoration, and I knew at that moment, in one heartbeat, Ethan would choose Damien every time. His heart belonged to his long-time partner and always would.

My heart seized once more, hurt crashing down over me, overshadowing the enthralled arousal the sight of the two men had brought to life inside my body. I bit my lip to keep quiet, but my emotions betrayed me.

Ethan's head jerked my way as though my pain reached out and slapped him across the face.

"Who the fuck are you?"

I jerked my focus to Damien's dark eyes, to the scowl turning down his full lips, seeing the beauty of him, and why Ethan couldn't say no.

"Shaylia," Ethan breathed my name, and I didn't need to have his abilities to recognize his own pain.

I couldn't look at him.

I spun, lower lip between my teeth to keep from crying, tears welling and hazing my vision as I grabbed my purse from beneath my desk and took off. Hurt had come in many forms throughout my life, betrayal by one I had trusted above all others.

Fool.

Tears coursed down my cheeks as I hurried into the bright, overhead sunlight shining down on the earth as though blessing me with her presence.

I stumbled to a stop on the sidewalk, overwhelmed and unable to think properly. I couldn't remember where I'd parked, couldn't decide if I ought to turn right or left, scurry away up a sidewalk, or flag the approaching cab.

A sob lodged in my throat, and I spun to the right, needing distance between the second man to crush my heart.

Chapter 15

Damien

I'd just blown my load with enough force to drop *me* to my knees, exhaustion from the long-ass flight from London loaded atop that temptation. Ethan's desire to please me, his accomplishment at doing so, his acceptance of my apology and agreeing to give us another chance filled me with bliss, fulfillment like I'd never known.

And one hot as fuck woman ripped it away within a mere second, yanking my focus back on reality.

"Who the fuck are you?" I asked, scowling while shoving my limp dick back in my pants.

She blinked, her wide blue eyes dominated by dark pupils—turned on from catching us in the middle of a blowjob. Tension flooded the room, hitching my shoulders.

Ethan whispered her name like a fucking prayer—like he used to do mine—and the dent between my brows deepened as he stared at her from his knees, his own shoulders slumped, pain etching *his* brow.

She spun and disappeared without a word.

"Goddamnit." Ethan shoved to his feet, his lips pursed, tucking his dick away.

"What's going on, Ethan?"

"She's the secretary from the temp agency. The one who started the same day you left," he explained without meeting my gaze and zippered up.

"And?"

Ethan closed his eyes and inhaled deeply, a shudder rippling through him. "It's a long story."

"Did you fuck her?"

"Yes." He opened his eyes, the fathomless greenish-hazel filled with a slew of emotions I wished I could feel.

My body trembled at his confession but not from exhaustion. I fought off my deepening scowl as I reminded myself I'd done the same behind his back. "It's okay," I forced out between clenched teeth.

"Goddamnit." Ethan ran his hand through his hair and glanced at the door. "She means something to me, Damien. I-I have to go talk to her." He strode off without another word, leaving me alone in his office.

I blinked, trying to process the previous handful of minutes, unsure if I should hold on to my hurt over his relationship with her or put it away since I had no right to feel betrayed. Hadn't I fucked a woman while in London? Hadn't I let her put her mouth on me, give her a mouthful of cum?

It had been Ethan on my mind while giving her that gift, but it had been her throat I'd emptied into.

"Fuck." I cursed a few more times, pulled at my messy hair, and glanced around the office. Everything sat in its usual place, unmoved, where it belonged—just like Ethan belonged in my life. Like I told him, without him, I couldn't imagine going on. I couldn't fathom a life where he wasn't beside me, one without his understanding, his acceptance.

I had always thought I'd been enough for Ethan—but I truly hadn't.

My throat tightened, and I strode into the bathroom and grabbed some towels to clean up the mess he'd made on his floor.

Ethan returned before I finished, his tie askew and hair mussed like mine as though he'd been running his hands through the dark strands. "She's gone."

He slumped in his chair, his head tipped back, eyes closed.

I stood a few feet away, cum-smeared paper towels wadded in my hand, at a loss for words.

"The first time I met her, I told her about the gallery I wanted to open. She seemed as excited for me as I was." Ethan swallowed, the bob of his Adam's apple slow as though he fought tears. "She supported me. Helped me set everything up."

"She gave you what I didn't."

"Yes." He met my stare, and I had to look away.

Sun shone through the window behind him, but I wished for the darkest night, a storm to match the one in my head.

"I'm confused as hell, Damien."

Ethan's whisper drew my focus back to his face. He stared at his hands, lying limp in his lap.

"I love you—I always have and always will, but I also want her." He lifted his focus, confusion in his eyes.

"You want us both."

Ethan blinked and jerked his head in a nod, as though realizing for the first time the truth of his words.

My initial impression of the woman named Shaylia certainly hadn't been one of disgust, but I'd been so caught up in my post climax, I couldn't remember much beyond the swell of perfectly sized breasts and blue eyes.

Even though Ethan and I had shared a few women on a whim in the past, I never considered bringing a third into our relationship for longer than one night. I'd always enjoyed the softness of a woman, but then again, Ethan had been more than enough for me, and I'd never felt the need for more in the long term.

"I'll do whatever you need me to do, Ethan," I reminded him, not turned off in the least by his thoughts about wanting us both. "But the way she hurried out of here…" I shrugged, doubting he had a chance of making things right with her.

He expelled another huge breath. "She probably hates my guts."

"You told her about us?"

"Yes."

"Our history?"

"Yes."

I mulled over the situation a bit as my brain began firing again or at least, with the circuits not wiped out from lack of sleep. "Find her. Tell her everything. Your thoughts, your feelings, your desires."

"Shit." Ethan pinched the bridge of his nose. "I wish I was more like my mom."

"Fuck that, Ethan." I scowled. "You're fucking perfect the way you are. Don't be spouting off shit about your life only having value when you help people. You went out and opened a gallery for yourself. Go find Shaylia and help *yourself* for a change if this is what you really want. If she won't accept you, won't allow you to help get over her disappointment or anger, then it's her loss."

My gain, I didn't add, seeing as how I'd promised to be a changed man.

Ethan nodded, letting out a heavy sigh, his focus slipping down over me. "Go home. Shower and crawl in bed."

I narrowed my eyes. "Is your bossing me around part of the new *us*?"

The corner of his lip twitched as though to smile, but it never appeared. "You would never allow me to top you."

I studied him long enough, he shifted beneath my stare.

"Things change," I murmured the reminder of what I'd told him twice—I was willing to do whatever he needed in order to be happy.

Lust flared to life in his eyes, along with the new stubborn determination I think I adored. My dick certainly did, twitching with the desire to swell again. I grinned and turned away instead, making for my office and the keys I'd tossed onto my desk.

"I need to shower and sleep. I'll see you later."

His groan thickened me fully, but I shut the door between our offices, grabbed my keys, and got my ass home before I passed out.

Chapter 16

Ethan

I caved into my feelings for Damien—caved to the lure of the past tying us together, the comfort of our connection, the promise of his desire to change things for the better.

But, as I told him, I still wanted Shaylia. She saw me, didn't judge, and supported me in ways no one ever had. Tossing her aside as though what we had shared in our short time together meant nothing wasn't right—and I sure as hell didn't want to.

The lancing pain I'd felt from her seconds after ejaculating while sucking Damien off, caved in my chest. Emotional upheaval had slammed into my head, into my heart, seizing my breath. I'd barely been able to whisper her name, finding her backed against my office door, staring at Damien.

She didn't even glance down at me.

Shame, guilt, heartache, feeling as though I'd betrayed her crippled me for long enough, I didn't rush after her the second she'd run off.

I stared at my office door as it closed behind Damien, half-hard again from his suggestion he might allow me to top him. The desire for both him and Shaylia tore my insides to shreds. I needed to set things right with her, but perhaps allowing her time to cool off and process might be best.

I grabbed my cell and stared, rather than typing, wanting to spill my guts, but also keep it short. I ended up somewhere in the middle and re-read my message three times before sending it off, my fingers crossed.

Me: **I know what you're feeling, and I'll understand if you never want to speak to me again, but what you and I have isn't something I'm ready to just toss away, Shaylia. Please allow me a chance to explain my heart.**

I stayed put in my office, hoping for a reply, trying to focus on work while my brain and heart threatened to shut down.

Madeline inquired about Shaylia shortly after returning from lunch, but I said she'd gone home sick. I hated lying but telling her Shaylia had walked in on me sucking Damien's dick wasn't an option, regardless of how long Madeline had been with the company.

While I felt sure most of those within our office knew about Damien's and my relationship, doing what we'd done in the middle of the day *shouldn't* have happened.

Trusting Madeline to lock up behind her at five, I headed out a half-hour early. Rather than head north to Shaylia's as my heart wanted me to, I followed my head and returned to our condo. Silence met me as I let myself in, and a quick glance around showed me Damien hadn't unpacked yet. Both suitcases sat beside the couch, and no light spilled from our ajar bedroom door.

I watched him sleep for a time, both arms beneath his pillow as he sprawled on his stomach. We'd hung light-blocking blinds, so I couldn't make out his form clearly, but I knew every dip, every swell of muscle along his back. My hands had gripped his ass countless times while he'd fucked mine.

My dick thickened, and I tore my attention off him, going into the bathroom. I imagined stripping off the emotions of the day while stepping out of my clothes, but they refused to fall to the floor as easily.

Hot water pelted my face, rinsing off the lather of soap, but the turmoil in my heart didn't swirl down the drain with the bubbles. Exhaustion pulled at me, and I didn't even bother with food once done in the shower.

Not yet six in the evening, I crawled into our bed, curling on my side to face Damien.

Lips parted, the skin between his brows smoothed out, he slept soundly. I closed my eyes, enjoying the silence, the lack of emotions beyond my own.

Eventually, I drifted off.

I woke before the sun, the scent of coffee coaxing my eyes open.

Damien stood in the bedroom doorway, his body backlit by the kitchen's light. His wide shoulders and trim waist along with the muscular thighs I loved having between mine prodded my dick awake.

Rolling to my back tented the sheet covering me, but Damien stayed put, sipping from a mug, his emotions ten times quieter than mine.

"Did you find her?" he asked quietly.

"I didn't go after her."

"Why not?"

"I decided she probably needed time, so I texted her, asking for a chance to explain once she was ready."

"Did she reply?"

"Not as of last night." I twisted to grab my cell off the bed stand and tapped the screen to life. "Not as of this morning, either." I tossed my cell back and exhaled a sigh, horny and heartsick.

Feeling sure Damien's emotions would lean toward pleased by Shaylia's dismissal, I blinked to find him calm. He moved toward me, placing his coffee beside my cell, and sat beside me on the bed's edge.

"I can't feel your emotions," he said, staring at me in the near dark, "but I know you must be hurting."

My chest tightened with love for him, for his empathetic thinking.

"Let me make you feel better," he murmured, leaning down, his fingers weaving through my hair.

I sighed as his lips met mine, unhurried and gentle for a change as though he wished to show me how tender, how loving he could be.

The lack of intimacy for over two weeks, however, didn't allow the sweetness to continue. Our kiss grew hungry, and I reached between his thighs, finding him hard, hot, and heavy against my hand.

"Please, Damien," I groaned against his demanding mouth, needing him inside me, connecting our souls as they ought to be.

He yanked open the bed stand drawer for lube while I ripped the sheet off me.

"I need to see you." Damien flicked on the light. "Need to see your eyes while I fuck you."

I drew my knees up as he settled between my thighs, his dark eyes penetrating mine as his lubed fingers did the same to my ass.

"Fuck me, Damien."

The broad head of his thick cock replaced his fingers as he quickly wiped his hand on the rumpled sheet beside his knee.

Time paused. Our breath sounded loud in my ears as we stared at one another. I felt his love, felt his need to show that love.

"Fill me," I told him.

He pushed in with a groan, seating his dick deep inside me, and I cursed at the sudden fullness, the sting of having gone without him for too long.

"Fuck, did I miss this ass." Damien planked over me, flexing and pulling out, shoving back in, only to retreat again. I fought to keep my eyes open, moaning with every glide of his length inside me. Every slickened slide, every grunt and thrust intensified the heat between us as he stared into my eyes.

Damien owned me in every way, and the second he wrapped his hand around my cock, jacking me with every thrust of his hips, I knew he would for the rest of our lives.

"Gonna come, Ethan," he groaned, squeezing my base. "Gonna fill your ass with my cum."

Buried deep, he grunted, and the first shot of heat inside my body erupted my balls, and ropes of my cum shot up toward my pecs.

My eyes clenched shut, head tipped back, caught up in release—but a part of me felt as though something was missing.

Shaylia.

Her name whispered in my head with the last twitch of my dick, and I sucked in air, guilt over thinking about her at that moment rising to sour my mood.

Damien collapsed on top of me, smearing my cum between us. "Were you thinking about her?"

Fuck. I clenched my eyes shut harder. "Not until the very end," I admitted—as if that made it any better.

The pain my confession caused him flitted over my mind, and I expected Damien to pull out, leaving me empty, but he didn't move his weight off me.

"I fucked a woman while I was in London."

His guilt slammed into me as though he'd let a wall down inside his head.

I clenched my eyes shut and swallowed against rising pain since I had no right to feel betrayed.

"There's no fucking excuse," he said, lifting to plank over me, his softening dick sliding from my ass, "so I won't offer one."

"I understand why you did it," I whispered, reaching up to touch his face. "It's okay."

"It's *not*," Damien said, his brow furrowing.

He climbed into the shower without another word, and I cursed myself a half-dozen times, lying there with my arm over my eyes.

He'd fucked a woman.

I'd fucked a woman—more than once.

We stood on even ground as far as betrayals went even if we had been broken up, but my transgression hadn't been a one-night stand.

Damien had promised to do anything for me, and I hated that I had forced our situation on us. I hated my desire for her hurt him—but I hated he would hurt himself by agreeing to share me in order to please me even more.

He'd seemed receptive to her joining us the day before, even suggesting it, but perhaps that wasn't what he truly wanted.

I stared at the closed bathroom door, and it wasn't until the water shut off I thought to check for a reply from Shaylia again.

No messages.

Fridays were usually my favorite day, but the idea of sitting in an office all day with Damien in the one beside me and Shaylia right outside my door clenched my stomach. Perhaps it would be best to pull her in the second I got there and lay it all out.

Without a shred of hope, I climbed out of bed, needing so much more than a mere cup of coffee.

Chapter 17

Shaylia

My insecurities of never being enough hadn't slammed me so hard since finding out my father had another family. Not since I was eight did the sour taste of self-doubt and self-worth plummet me into hell.

I hadn't been enough for my dad—he'd gone off and got himself another wife, one with a son I refused to hear anything about. I wasn't the boy he must have always wanted.

Falling short became a way of life, and it revealed itself yet again as I compared myself to Damien Fiorenza and found myself sorely lacking. He was a rich, handsome man, powerful and successful. He also had a dick, something I used to lament not having when thinking my father had wanted a son rather than a daughter.

Not enough.

I soaked my pillow, hardly sleeping all night as thoughts of falling short of what Ethan wanted and needed haunted my mind. Climbing out of bed Friday morning didn't come easy, and even my coffee held no joy, no taste.

For the first time in my life, I called in sick to work. Madeline didn't answer—the office hadn't yet opened—but I left a message to let her know not to expect me. I had no clue what Ethan had told her the day before about my disappearance, and I couldn't find it in myself to care.

I ate a pint of cherry vanilla ice cream and drank a bottle of wine for dinner rather than eat food. More tears, endless tissues, and a sore nose from blowing it all day plagued me, and I fell into bed, feeling just as shitty as the day before.

Saturday, the pain seemed less when I woke, and I actually felt like showering. Damp hair hanging down my back and wetting my over-sized t-shirt, I shuffled into the kitchen for a third cup of coffee, vowing to get out into the sunshine and breathe in the fresh summer air. I needed to cleanse my lungs, cleanse my mind. Make a plan to move on in my quest to be the best *me* I could.

I couldn't afford to go back to school, but I would find a secretarial job where I would be appreciated for my outstanding skills. I vowed to never date again, never open my heart to possible hurt, never trust anyone with a dick, no matter how sincere and kind they might seem.

A knock on my door clenched my eyes shut.

He's not all to blame.

Cursing at the angel on my shoulder, I yanked open my door without checking out the window, knowing who stood on my stoop.

Ethan hovered, hands shoved in his pockets, shoulders hunched.

My breath caught at the instant energy rippling between us, the desire to feel his arms around me.

"What do you want?" I managed to whisper, my hand in a death grip on the door's handle to keep from shaking, wrapping my other arm around my middle.

"I need to explain. Please."

I considered slamming the door in his face. I reminded myself of the vow from moments before about not trusting again.

I found myself stepping back to let him in because I couldn't stand seeing Ethan in pain.

Fool.

Lips pursed, I shut the door behind him and moved toward the coffee pot. "Coffee?"

"Please."

I managed to not spill any coffee and set the full mug on the table before sitting across from it, heart in my throat, my pulse thrumming.

Ethan settled into the other chair and enclosed the mug with his long fingers before meeting my gaze. "Damien came back sooner than expected."

I didn't say a word, simply sipped coffee I couldn't taste.

Ethan glanced down at the steam rising from his mug. "He's willing to change his ways, willing to be the man he feels I need in order to be fulfilled."

Whatever hope my subconscious had allowed shattered into dozens of cutting shards, and I bit my lip to keep more tears from spilling.

"Being near him again, feeling his love, his desire to be everything I need undid me, Shaylia. I love him. I always have and always will."

Ethan finally looked at me again, and I fought off the tears, swallowing the thickness in my throat.

"But…" his whisper faded off as his focus dropped to my mouth. "But when I saw you standing by the door, the reality of you slammed into me—all your hurt, your disappointment—and I realized the last thing I wanted in this life is to hurt you."

"Don't pity me, Ethan," I whispered.

"I don't." He peered into my eyes, leaning forward with his elbows on the table. "I want you."

My heart skipped, and I blinked. "What do you mean?"

"I love Damien, but I want more. *Need* more in my life."

I shivered under his intense stare and licked the sudden dryness from my lips. "You're … choosing *me*?"

He hesitated from answering, confusing the ever loving hell out of my head.

"Please don't play games, Ethan," I said, my voice hoarse and shaking, my hands clutching my mug. "Just tell me the truth."

"I need Damien like I need to fill my lungs without thought—but I also need you like a plant needs sunlight, needs rain to grow."

The reality of what he said took a few seconds to slam into my brain. "You want us both."

I didn't voice a question, but he nodded, his hazel-green eyes imploring me to understand. My emotions ran amuck, riotous at the thought he wished to do to Damien as my father had to my mother.

"I will not be your secret lover," I said, my voice hard, yet still shaking. "I will not be the woman on the side you go to when Damien isn't enough."

"That's not what I mean—"

I shot to my feet, my entire body trembling. "I told you what my father did to us, and you have the balls to think of doing the same to Damien?" My voice rose, bordering on hysteria.

"No. Please—"

"Get out."

Ethan stood, reaching for me, but I stepped back, holding up my hand to keep him away.

"I can't believe I trusted you." My voice caught. "I can't believe what you're suggesting!" Tears coursed down my cheeks as I fought to align the Ethan I'd known the previous three weeks to the one spewing shit at my kitchen table.

"You didn't let me finish." He frowned, his arm dropping to his side.

"So finish," I all but spat the words, wrapping my arms under my breasts, trying like hell to hold myself together when all I wanted was for him to go away so I could drown my sorrows in wine.

"I want you both. Together. All three of us sharing a life —not separate or secretive. I would never suggest such a thing to you of all people, Shaylia. Ever."

My mind blanked for a moment, but images and thoughts roared to life a second later, and I blinked as the waterworks in my eyes eased. Him and Damien. And me. Both men *with* me. "A-A threesome?"

"It's terribly selfish of me to ask this of you, Shaylia, but I *can't* choose one of you over the other. I can't. I need you both, our sharing a life equally among all three. I know it's not conventional, but it can work."

"You can't be serious." Hysterical laughter rose like champagne bubbles.

"I am."

"And what does your partner think of that idea?" Not that I cared what Damien thought, but I found myself wondering.

"He's willing to do whatever it takes to make me happy."

My body sagged as the reality of Damien's love for Ethan fell over me. I didn't stand a chance with that kind of love. "He would share you."

"Yes."

"With a woman he doesn't even know."

"He'll get to know you, Shaylia." Ethan took a step toward me, but I didn't back off. "He'll adore you the same as I do. I know he will."

"You're mad. Crazy."

Ethan held my stare, tension once more rippling between us. "I need you, and I'm not beyond getting on my knees to beg you to give the three of us a chance."

My heartbeat kicked back into high gear, and I squeezed myself tighter as thoughts of watching him and Damien again—with their knowledge of an audience—heated my core. I remembered Damien's tipped back head as he'd come in Ethan's mouth, the veins rising along his neck as he strained, groaning his release.

I'd never seen anything so hot in my life.

Moisture coated my panties, and my nipples pebbled.

If nothing else, the devil whispered, *you'll experience a threesome. Two men at once. What woman doesn't want that?*

You could be left doubly broken, the angel argued.

"Shaylia?"

I blinked, pulling myself back to my kitchen.

"Would you at least agree to meet Damien? Give friendship, to start, a chance?"

Oh, how I wanted to say yes.

"There's no pressure," Ethan said when I didn't reply, and I knew he felt my desire … and my hesitancy. "You'll be in control of how things transpire. Nothing physical will happen unless you want it to."

Damien loved Ethan enough to give him what he wanted. I didn't love him—yet I didn't believe—but the thought of making Ethan happy, of seeing the joy I'd been a part of while setting up his gallery swayed me.

"Okay," I whispered, not bothered by having to share him, which baffled the hell out of me.

"Okay?"

I nodded, and Ethan's smile lightened his face, his eyes glowing the color of grass in springtime.

He moved forward, arms raising as though to hug me, but I backed against the counter. His happiness faded, his smile unsteady. "Okay."

"When?" I asked, hugging myself again.

"Tonight? I can pick you up."

I shook my head. "Just tell me where to meet you."

He pursed his lips for a moment as though thinking. "Would you come to our condo?"

I considered the conversation ahead of us and recognized the need for privacy. "Yes."

Hope flooded his face, but I forced myself in check from responding as my heart and body wanted to. He left a moment later, and legs once more weakened at the enormity of what had transpired, I slumped back in my chair.

"*You're* the crazy one," I mumbled.

So much for vows and self-control. I almost hated myself for caving, and if it weren't for Ethan's happiness, I very well might have cursed myself to hell.

Chapter 18

Damien

Ethan had turned away from my advances Friday night, and I'd stared into the dark long after he'd slept.

Shaylia hadn't shown for work, and he'd moped all day, making me jealous enough, my stomach churned. Jealousy wasn't an emotion I'd dealt with before because I'd never doubted Ethan's love. Finding out I was no longer enough to fulfill him stung like a bitch, but I'd promised to do anything. If keeping Ethan meant I needed to accept someone else in our bed, I could deal.

I woke early Saturday morning and went for a run along the river, soaking in the rising sun, the city's waking, and the sounds of traffic. With every thump of my feet and every beat of my heart, I thought of Ethan, of what we shared, all we would share in our future if I kept my selfishness contained.

Trusting Shaylia, no matter what Ethan claimed about her, wouldn't come easy, but I told myself I would try. If she wasn't the type of woman who played games, we might settle in easier. Knowing Ethan would better discern her intentions eased my anxiety but only slightly.

I didn't like the thought of sharing him—his love and adoration, his attention and laughter—but I wasn't one to break promises.

Ethan wasn't at home when I got back to the condo. I'd left him sleeping, his mug ready by the coffee pot. He left me a note on the table, his mug unused as though he'd been in a hurry to get out the door. Soaked in sweat and still breathing heavy, I grabbed the blue sticky note.

I'm going to talk to Shaylia.

He hadn't texted because I never took my phone when I ran in the morning. I crumpled the paper in my hand, trying like fuck not to be jealous, not to overthink how he'd ignored me in bed the night before and ran off to her the second I'd left the condo.

I grabbed my earbuds and cell, and headed downstairs to our building's weight room to blow off my rising steam while hurting my ears with some screaming metal.

* * *

Ethan sat on the couch when I returned a couple of hours later, his back to me while he watched the news.

I tossed my earbuds and cell onto the table and rounded the couch, thankful I'd exhausted my pissiness. "How'd it go?" I asked, standing beside him, a soaked and stinking mess.

"She's coming over for dinner." He glanced up at me— probably waiting to experience whatever emotion rode me.

Feeling rather numb, I nodded, pleased over keeping my cool. "I'll be on my best behavior. Put on the charm."

"I'd rather if you were yourself, Damien."

Hands on my hips, I peered down at him.

"I want her to know you, the real Damien, the man I love. No games, no suave lines to get in her pants for my sake, okay?"

I dipped my head. "You got it."

"I'm nervous as hell," he said, his voice low, wiping his palms down his jeans.

"Afraid I'll scare her off?"

"No. I'm more afraid she won't be physically attracted to you enough to give this a shot."

"Fuck. You're saying I'm not all that?"

"Cocky asshole." He snorted. "I'm just saying, what if there isn't a connection?"

"It was me she stared at Thursday morning," I said, trying not to chuckle. "Her pupils dilated and lips parted while you sucked my cock."

"Seeing us together is what turned her on," Ethan grumbled his argument.

"We'll see," I said with a grin, turning toward the bathroom and a long-ass shower.

"And what about your first impression?" Ethan called to me.

I paused in our bedroom doorway and glanced over my shoulder. "She's hot as fuck, from what I saw, so getting it up won't be an issue if that's what she wants."

He rolled his eyes.

"What?" I pushed, my lips twitching, happiness over our banter lightening the heaviness in my heart.

"Getting it up has never been an issue for you."

"What can I say?" My grin reappeared as I stretched out my arms. "I'm a fucking god."

Chapter 19

Ethan

I'd never been so damn nervous in my life. Damien felt close to the same, but he pretended not to. He'd always been good at putting on a front, one of unruffled confidence I envied. His hurt over what I'd done while he'd been away lingered though.

That, too, he tried to ignore.

The Red Sox game finished up the bottom of the seventh, and I stood from the couch, empty wine glass in hand. "Want another?" I asked him, motioning toward his glass.

"I'll wait for dinner." He glanced at his watch. "She's late."

Lips pursed, I turned toward the kitchen. "She'll be here."

He grunted and muttered—and the doorbell rang.

My heart spasmed, and I set my wine glass on the counter and hurried to the front door as Damien changed the game to a music channel and lowered the volume.

The sight of Shaylia's wobbly smile, the overflow of anxiety rolling off her kicked my empathy into high gear. Seeing how she clutched her purse in front of her like a shield, I stepped back rather than hug her as I desperately wanted to.

"Thanks for coming." I smiled, hoping to ease her a bit but failed.

She moved into the entryway, and Damien's footfalls sounded behind me as I shut the door.

She stared up at him as I turned. Having two inches on my six-foot height, he towered over most, the width of his shoulders and prominent pectorals beneath his tight t-shirt intimidating and hot as hell.

If she wasn't turned on by his appearance, she was an ice goddess—and I was doomed.

Enough anxiety and tension rose among us, I struggled to find my voice. "Shaylia, this is Damien. Damien, Shaylia."

"It's nice to finally meet you," Damien said, holding out his hand, appreciation for her looks in his eyes.

She nodded and slipped her hand into his. "You, too," she whispered, the pulse in her neck thrumming—I hoped from arousal rather than just the nerves tensing her shoulders.

Damien's easy smile—a real one—twinkled his dark eyes. "Ethan has been singing your praises, but he hasn't done your beauty justice."

Shaylia's cheeks flushed, and I rolled my eyes even though pleasure that they seemed to be attracted to one another coursed through me.

"Can I get you a glass of wine?" I asked her, stepping past them into the kitchen.

"Please." She followed me, her anxiety lessening the slightest bit.

Since she'd enjoyed her pasta from our first date, I'd thrown together a quick marinara, not thinking perhaps she might be too nervous to eat—I knew I sure as hell was.

Damien held out his hand again, and she gave him her purse, her back turning toward me to do so. Denim capris hugged her ass and thighs, and even though I'd promised no sexual advances, my dick took interest. I got a semi before I could force my focus to pouring her wine.

"Hungry?" Damien asked her.

"A little."

I turned to find he had pulled out a chair at the table, but she didn't sit immediately.

"I'm not here for sex," she said, her tone low and shaking, staring up at Damien. "I'm here to get to know the man Ethan loves, the one I'll need to share him with to make him happy."

Damien's smile softened, his sincerity and his confidence easing the tension riding my shoulders. "All I want is to make him happy, too, Shaylia. If that means being your friend, I can do that. If that means eventually being your lover, I certainly won't complain about that either."

Pink infused her cheeks again, and she slid onto the chair, her focus on the plate before her. The pulse in her neck jumped, and the image of the three of us together in our bed thickened my dick fully.

"Wine." I held out her glass, and she finally looked me full in the eyes as though wanting to see me for the first time that night.

The corner of her lip tugged upward—and didn't wobble.

My smile came easy as a flash of hope hit me square in the chest.

Damien sat beside her. "Let's cut to the chase, Shaylia."

"O-okay?"

"We're here to get to know each other, so we're going to play twenty questions."

Her brow furrowed for a split second.

"No games," Damien said, holding her gaze, "but a means of laying a foundation I want, and I'm pretty sure you do as well."

Shaylia glanced between us, but I couldn't read her face. "Are you always the one in charge?" she asked, turning back toward Damien.

A glint lit his eye, and I realized they had begun.

I dished up our pasta as he chuckled.

"I always used to be," Damien admitted, "but recent events have made me realize I can't control everything —which I fucking hate if we're honest."

"I'll never be controlled," Shaylia stated with such finality, my focus jerked to Damien's face.

Lust flared to life in his eyes, and my dick throbbed, knowing his did as well with the need to conquer. He let the topic go, however, tossing out the next question —why she was willing to share me with him.

"Because I want to make him happy." She glanced at me, and I swore love emanated from her eyes even if that emotion didn't reach out from her to caress me. "Same as you," she added, turning back to Damien.

They continued their twenty-questions, leaning toward the usual get-to-know you type of conversation a couple on their first date might gravitate toward.

I'd already learned Shaylia was an only child, and that her father had left her and her mom when she'd been eight. While eating, she stated the facts, not holding anything back, even about how she struggled to find self-worth after he'd abandoned her. I couldn't have been more pleased to hear her open up, willing to let Damien inside her personal life.

He, however, held quite a bit back, only briefly mentioning his stepfather and how the man had ruined his grandfather's business and name. He focused on how I had helped him rebuilt his grandfather's empire, how much he leaned on me in all things.

"No wonder you're willing to do anything to make him happy," Shaylia said, peering at Damien as he pushed his plate away and reached for his wine.

His gaze narrowed. "Meaning?"

"He's given up his dreams for your family name—for *you*."

"He did."

"So, is it love or the need to repay him that made you agree to this?" she asked, motioning around the table.

Damien's emotions didn't play out on his face, but his annoyance *and* his appreciation of her trying to call him out feathered through my mind. I bit my tongue to keep from smiling, knowing he hoped to one day own her even if he wouldn't ever want to tame her spunk.

"It's both," he finally said, his dark eyes taking on a twinkle. "I owe him my life, and I'll gladly give it if that's what he needs from me."

"Glad to hear it." Shaylia didn't smile. Sipping her wine, she glanced at me. "So…"

I raised an eyebrow but kept silent.

"What exactly do *you* want, Ethan? Where would this go if you have your way?"

A deep inhale filled my lungs. "I love Damien—always have and always will—but you own a piece of me, Shaylia." I picked up her hand resting on the table, and she didn't pull away as I laced my fingers through hers. "Right or wrong, I don't care. I want you both."

"You want to date both of us."

I stared into her blue eyes, hoping she could see how much I loved him, how far I'd fallen for her, needed her, too. "Yes."

"You want to sleep with both of us." Her low voice and heightened pulse in her smooth neck once more brought hope to my heart.

"Preferably at the same time," I murmured, holding her stare.

She didn't speak as her excitement and hesitancy mingled between us.

The opening bars of Adele's playing *Make You Feel My Love* sounded quietly from the TV, and the need to feel her in my arms, to show her how much she belonged there persuaded me to push a bit.

"Dance with me?" I asked, squeezing her fingers and standing.

She followed along without pause, settling her cheek against my chest when I tugged her toward me once we stood in the living room.

Damien followed us and settled on the couch with his wine. He studied us, sipping as we swayed to the purity of Adele's piano playing and angelic voice.

The scent of vanilla filled my nose as I buried my face in her hair. Softness laid beneath my hands, and I fought the desire to roam, mapping out the curves I'd memorized, the lushness of her body I dreamed about. My heart ached to hold her closer, tell her there wasn't anything I wouldn't do for her.

Damien shifted on the couch, drawing my focus.

The bulge between his spread thighs told me all I needed to know on his end—the horny fucker.

Another slow love song started where Adele's ended, and deciding to push a bit more, I pulled Shaylia tight against me, allowing her to feel how much I wanted her.

She sighed and melted against me as my hard length pressed into her belly.

We swayed through a second song, the sexual tension between us growing with every exhale, every beat of our hearts. By the time the third song began, I had decided to give her a chance to shut us down and motioned Damien over with my head.

He set his wine aside without hesitation and moved close to us. "Can I join you?" he asked, his rumbled tone shivering Shaylia and jerking my dick in my jeans.

Shaylia lifted her head to peer over her shoulder, her nerves once more making an appearance. "Is it what you want Ethan?" she asked, turning her focus on my face.

"Only if you do."

She nibbled her lower lip for a few seconds, but nodded, easing my breath.

Damien stepped close behind her, his hands resting atop mine on her hips—but he kept his body a few inches away.

"Okay?" I asked, drawing Shaylia's focus up to my face again, my heart in my damn throat at the size of her pupils.

She nodded again, sending a rush of air from my lungs and a smear of pre-cum over the inside of my boxers.

I met Damien's gaze over her head. Lust darkened his eyes, but the love I felt radiating from him soothed me. The three of us hadn't yet connected in the way I hoped, in the way Damien obviously wanted as much as me, but touching them both at the same time, their influx of emotions, however spiked or riotous, righted my world.

Chapter 20

Shaylia

Seeing Ethan on his knees Thursday morning—upon later reflection—had let me know for sure who the dominant party was in their relationship. Being in Damien's personal space confirmed my thoughts, and I understood Ethan's inability to say no to the man. He exuded authority, power in a way I'd never known in a person before.

Self-assured and confident but not in an overbearing or cocky manner like most would be in his position. While speaking over dinner, I didn't get the feeling he wanted to play games either, which was why I decided to confront him on why he'd agreed to meet me. I'd expected a scowl of annoyance, but he surprised me by showing his appreciation for my questioning his motive.

Feeling as though we understood one another lessened my nervousness, my concern on feeling out what Ethan declared he wanted from both of us—*with* both of us.

While not the norm, by any means, the thought of a threesome came easier since Damien intrigued me enough, I wouldn't mind testing the waters. The fact my hormones responded to his hot as hell body and gorgeous face, growing all warm and tingling inside, certainly made the decision easier.

I stared up at Ethan as he asked me if I was okay, and knowing I stood on the brink of a cliff, the bottom far from sight, I hesitated before nodding.

His hold on my waist tightened as he squeezed, his smile flooding my heart. He glanced over my head—at Damien behind me—and I wondered at the silent communication between them.

Ethan returned his focus to me, to my mouth and released one hand on my hip to slide up to cradle the back of my head as Damien's hand settled where his had vacated. "Can I kiss you?"

Damien's touch singed through my capris, and I swallowed a rush of saliva as my heart pounded in my ears. "Yes."

I wondered at my need to hurry, to rise to my tiptoes to close the distance between us, but couldn't help myself. I'd missed him, his touch more than I'd thought. The softness, the gentle caress of his lips lightened my head and nearly caved my chest in with the depletion of anxiety.

Zero doubt I belonged to Ethan raged through my body, heightening my already racing pulse. I grabbed hold of his head and sank into him as he slid his tongue into my mouth, weakening my knees.

The brush of Damien against my back raced fire over my skin, pebbling every inch, exposed and beneath clothing. A shift of my hips pressed my ass against his thighs, and he groaned as his hard length rubbed against my lower back.

Forget fire—lava rushed through my veins, and I shuddered, pulling away from Ethan's mouth, gasping for breath. "I-I've never done this before," I somehow managed to say before trembling took over my body.

"We'll take things slow," Ethan whispered, brushing my hair back from my face.

"*If* that's what you want," Damien added, the heat of his breath lifting the hairs on my nape.

I bit back a moan as he sandwiched me fully between the two men, tempting all thought to flutter from my mind. My head tipped back onto Damien's shoulder as I fought to slow my pulse, to catch my breath. He leaned in and kissed Ethan right beside my face.

Kissed Ethan … inches from my face.

Both groaned, and my core liquefied as I stared at their hungry mouths, tongues, and teeth, appearing in flashes as they devoured one another, grinding against me as though I was a conduit between their bodies.

All strength left me, and I sagged between their hardness, my pussy pulsing, thighs squeezing to ease the ache in my clit. I bit my lip at Ethan's moan, his surrender to Damien's hold on his hair and control of the kiss.

I'd said I hadn't come to their condo for sex, but hell if I could think of anything else at that moment.

Damien pulled back too damn soon, and Ethan panted, the darkness of his pupils dominating the green of his eyes. Damien released his hold on Ethan's hair and ran his hands up and down my sides, his thumbs brushing the sides of my breasts, his hot breath once more caressing my neck—my ear.

"Ready to call it a night, Shaylia?" he murmured.

"No," I didn't hesitate to answer.

"What do you want?" His whisper shivered over my skin.

The memory of him coming undone while Ethan had knelt before him wiggled me between them. I wanted to see that look on his face again, the beautiful sight of a powerful man losing himself to the one he loved.

"I want to watch," I whispered, my heart pounding so damn hard, I wondered if it would stutter to a stop.

Damien stepped away, grasping my hand, tugging me from Ethan's hold to follow him. My legs shook, pulse raced.

I glanced over my shoulder to find Ethan adjusting himself through his jeans, his gaze on my ass. He lifted his focus and started after us, the happiness in his eyes filling my heart. I stumbled and turned, bumping into Damien's back as he paused to turn on the dimmer lights in their bedroom.

The king-sized bed sat against the far wall, and I stared at it, arms wrapping around my waist as Damien dragged a rounded arm chair to the bed's edge.

"Front-row seat." He patted the back, a wicked glint in his eyes.

Sexy, sexy man...

Swallowing, I dropped into the chair, and he gathered my hair in one of his large hands, bending to rub his nose across the back of my neck, sending a shiver of goosebumps in his touch's wake.

"Anything specific you wish to see?" he asked against my ear as I stared at Ethan near the foot of the bed. Ethan ripped his shirt off overhead, flooding my mouth with drool.

"Show me how you love him," I told Damien.

"Gladly." He dropped my hair and strode toward Ethan.

The removal of clothing was a rushed affair. I stared, wishing to commit to memory every hurried movement between the two men. They freed one another from the confines of their jeans, both groaning and shuddering as their hands closed over each other's jutting cocks.

Appreciation for their hard, sculpted bodies, their long, thick lengths, straining and leaking, rippled another shudder through me. My hips shifted on their own, and I clutched my hands on my lap to keep from touching myself through my capris.

"On the bed," Damien murmured against Ethan's mouth before one last nip on his lower lip.

Ethan crawled across the mattress and laid on his back, glancing my way, but I couldn't tear my gaze from his cock and the emptiness between my thighs it brought to mind.

I'd always thought when men fucked, it would be doggy style, but seeing Damien settle between Ethan's legs, working himself with lube he'd retrieved from the bed stand, my eyes opened in a whole new way. He released his glistening length and reached between Ethan's thighs, holding his gaze as Ethan's back arched off the bed.

I stared as Damien fingered Ethan, gulped when he held the base of his cock and positioned it against

Ethan's ass. A flex of his ass cheeks moved him forward. Both men groaned, and my lungs and mouth agreed as I squirmed on the chair, my focus glued to Damien's cock sliding in and out of Ethan's ass.

"Touch yourself, Shaylia." Damien's low murmur as he sank deep into Ethan's body had my hand sliding between my thighs without hesitation.

So much for not being controlled.

Wetness soaked clear through my panties, dampening the crotch of my capris.

Damien pulled out and turned toward me. "Touch yourself the way you want to," he ordered and thrust into Ethan who grasped the comforter, whimpering. "Don't be ashamed of your needs."

My fingers shook, but I managed to undo the button and slide down my zipper, my attention flicking to Ethan.

He watched me as well, the green of his eyes all but eaten by his pupils.

I shifted down a bit on the chair for better access, sliding my hand into my panties, gasping as my fingertips slid over my throbbing clit.

Ethan's gaze dropped to my crotch, and a rush of wetness seeped from me, coating my fingers as he groaned.

"Show us how wet you are," Damien said, and I did as told, holding my hand up. "Fuck…" He thrust into Ethan, hard. "Did she taste sweet, Ethan?" he asked, his tone ragged as he thrust again.

"So damn sweet," Ethan moaned and sucked his lower lip between his teeth.

"Do you want to taste her while I fuck you?"

My gaze shot to Damien, who stared at me with a cocky grin, tempting me like the devil himself.

"Sit on his face, Shaylia. It's what Ethan wants … it'll make him *happy*."

The memory of Ethan's tongue, his mouth on my pussy, bringing me to climax rushed arousal through me to the point, I whimpered. Damien's smirk, his command should have irked me, but I couldn't find a single damn to give. Even though I said I wanted to watch, I wanted to be a part of what they shared.

I needed release.

I stripped out of my pants and panties, and Ethan reached for me as I climbed onto the bed. Holding Damien's gaze as he continued to thrust into Ethan's ass, I settled my pussy where he'd told me to.

Ethan's groan as he devoured me with his soft mouth and his probing tongue slammed my eyelids shut, and I lost all thought, giving over to my body's need to ride his face.

Chapter 21

Damien

Fuck, Shaylia was gorgeous when she relaxed and let go—her head tipped back, blue eyes hidden behind her eyelids and fluttering black lashes as she writhed atop Ethan's face, chasing her climax. Her chest heaved, raising her breasts with every inhale, her hot as fuck moans and whimpers taking me too damn close to blowing my load in Ethan's ass before I wanted to.

I dropped my focus to Ethan's bobbing, leaking dick, and grabbed hold of him while burying myself balls deep into his body again. I smeared his pre-cum down his length while dragging back out, and began the rhythm he loved, fucking his dick with my grip while shoving mine hard and deep into his ass.

He grasped at her thighs, his face hidden from me, but I knew without looking into his eyes, he neared the edge. I needed to push him over, but I wanted to connect with Shaylia, too.

"Kiss me, Shay."

She lifted her head and blinked her eyelids open, passion hazing and devouring the blue of her eyes as she writhed against Ethan's mouth.

I leaned forward on one arm, still working Ethan's dick and his ass, a challenge in my eye. "Kiss me," I repeated.

Ethan moaned, and she leaned toward me, her focus dropping to my mouth.

I swooped in and kissed her. Fucking ate at her mouth—the first woman I'd kissed since the seventh grade. Fuck, she tasted like cherries and wine, a sinful buffet, and I suddenly understood why Ethan hadn't been able to let her go.

Addictive and sweet, sexy as fuck with just enough spunk to make me dream of taming her ass, Shaylia fit me ... fit *us*.

"Come all over his face," I murmured, my teeth catching her lower lip.

Her breath hitched, and my fucking balls exploded as she shuddered, her cry releasing my hold on her mouth. Eyes wide, she stared at me while coming, the second spurt of my cum in Ethan's ass, the hard yank of my grip on his dick sending him over.

The sounds of wet lapping, moaning, and grunts as all three of us finished turned me on even as the last bit of cum eased from my dick.

I stilled, buried deep in Ethan's ass, rubbing my thumb over his soaked slit, sending another shudder through him.

The haze over Shaylia's eyes faded as she panted, and she blinked twice, eyes still wide as she stared at me.

I considered a few cheesy lines to toss out and discarded every one since they wouldn't explain what I felt. Pulling out of Ethan's ass, I nodded beside him. "Lie down, Shaylia, and let me take care of you."

She slumped onto the mattress, limbs askew, and I looked down at Ethan. Face flushed, her cream on his lips, he glanced between the two of us. Palming the head of my dick and grinning, I turned my back on them and went to the bathroom to clean up.

When I returned with wet towels for both of them, she snuggled against his side, her eyes closed, seemingly okay and peaceful. Ethan looked like the cat who swallowed a little birdie.

I cleaned her first, and she didn't do more than sigh and spread her legs a bit wider, allowing me to care for her. I always cared for Ethan after we fucked, considered it my duty as the dominant one. Doing so always filled me with gratification, with thankfulness for his willingness to offer his body for my release.

"Wine?" I asked, tossing the towels aside. Both focused on me—blue and green eyes alike—and nodded.

In nothing more than my skin, I strode out to the kitchen. Our dishes still sat on the table, the remnants of Ethan's kick-ass marinara on the stove. Ignoring the mess, I ran through what I'd learned of Shaylia while at the table, and while I'd appreciated what seemed to be her candid words, I wondered if she had an angle.

Didn't everyone?

My brow furrowed as the question rang in my head.

She held power over Ethan, that was obvious, and the possibility she might hurt him in the long run brought up my wary walls. Ethan had fallen to vulnerability with Shaylia, so it would be up to me to keep from doing the same to keep us both safe—just in case.

I would be the watch dog, staying in the right frame of mind should I find out she fucked us for something more than Ethan's happiness.

I returned to the bedroom, balancing three glasses of wine in my hands. No weirdness filled the silence among us as I handed them glasses and sat on the seat Shaylia had vacated, but Ethan had to feel the unsettled emotions in my mind.

Shaylia kept glancing between us, sitting against the headboard, her shirt still in place—panties retrieved from the floor and covering her bare pussy I definitely wanted to taste.

"How are you feeling, Shay?" I asked since I didn't have the abilities Ethan did. He seemed relaxed as well, lounging beside her. Without words though, I'd be left in the dark.

"Warm and tingling," she finally answered.

I chuckled, but she didn't smile at her confession. "Warm and tingling looks good on you," I murmured, noting the hard nipples poking from her shirt before turning my focus back up to her face.

Pink stained her cheeks, and Ethan shifted closer to her, laying his free hand on her thigh, lightly rubbing the smooth, pale skin.

"You're not upset things went this far," he said—I expected for my benefit.

"No." Her attention flitted my way again, and I smiled for real, realizing again why Ethan had fallen for her. Blue eyes, clear as a cloudless sky peered at me as though she could read through me as easily as Ethan's empath abilities could.

"And what about you, Damien?" she asked, her head tipping to the side. "Did it bother you to share him with me?"

"Not one fucking bit." I didn't bother hiding my grin and sipped my wine. I thought of telling her I could go for round two if she wanted, but her mouth opened first.

"I wasn't expecting this to happen tonight. Didn't plan on it," she said, glancing over at Ethan.

"Regrets?" he asked and sipped his wine.

She glanced at me and back to him. "Not really, no."

"But?"

Shaylia tore her focus off his face and studied the untouched wine in her hands. "The two of you have something very special. What if things progress but don't work out?" She swallowed. "I-I don't want to come between you."

I nearly groaned. "What if we *want* you between us?" I asked, keeping my voice conversational, all hint of lust hidden from my tone.

Shaylia gulped and glanced at me, the pulse kicking up in her neck. "You know what I meant, Damien."

"I do." I allowed a wicked glint in my eyes. "And I think you know what *I* meant."

She blinked, her lips parted.

"Well?" I pushed because … why the hell not?

Ensnared by my stare, she didn't glance away, the tip of her tongue flicking out to wet her lower lip. "Well, what?" she whispered.

She wanted me to spell it out—no problem. "Have you ever taken two men at the same time?"

She shook her head, her pupils swelling.

My dick twitched to life, but I refrained from working my length as it swelled between my thighs, drawing Shaylia's attention. "We would make it good for you."

Indecision warred on her face, but the way she'd given over to my earlier commands, how her body had responded to both Ethan and me swayed me into moving forward.

I stood, setting my wine on the bed stand. I held out my hands for their glasses—and only Shaylia hesitated a moment longer than Ethan before handing hers over.

"Lie back down, Ethan," I said, holding Shaylia's uncertain stare, expecting what I planned would create her need to give in fully. Keeping my focus on her eyes, I laid between Ethan's thighs and took his flaccid dick into my mouth.

"Oh." She blinked rapidly and squeezed her thighs together.

Score, I thought, focusing on making my man hard again, to ready his dick to slide into her sweet pussy.

Chapter 22

Ethan

Shaylia stared at Damien, her lips parted, as he coaxed my dick to full mast. She'd confessed to me weeks ago she hadn't known many lovers, and the excitement radiating off her from what she witnessed only intensified my own arousal. That and the fact I wasn't usually on the receiving end of a blowjob.

I fought the need to grab hold of Damien's head and fuck into his throat with abandon. I fought my desire to grab Shaylia and kiss her senseless while he worked me over. Damien backed off my dick with a pop, and I groaned as my dick sprang up to hit my abs.

"You have too many clothes on," he murmured, a devil of darkness in his eyes as he slid his gaze down over her.

She'd hesitated to hand over her wine, but she didn't at his suggestion, pulling her shirt off and unclasping her bra, freeing her breasts.

"Fuck," Damien groaned, and I wondered over his liking a woman's breasts. He'd never seemed interested before, but Shaylia's fullness, the darkened nipples straining for attention caught his attention.

"Ride him," he said, his tone one I never argued with.

Pussy lips glistening with arousal, Shaylia straddled me, ensnaring me with her wide eyes. I held my dick up, and she lowered, her lip between her teeth while penetrating herself on me. Damien crowded close against her back, his lips on the side of her neck, his hands testing the weight of her breasts.

"God, Shaylia," I groaned as she bottomed out against my groin. Tight, wet heat clamped around me, and I fought my eyes' need to roll back into my head at her sheer perfection.

"Ride him," Damien repeated in her ear, and she shuddered, her eyelids fluttering closed as he squeezed her nipples between his fingers.

I gripped her hips, merely holding while she rocked forward, dragging her clit along my lower abs before sliding back again, taking every inch of my dick.

"Does he feel good?" Damien asked, backing off.

"Yes," she whispered, her brow furrowed.

Damien met my gaze as he reached once more for the lube he'd left on the bed stand. I knew what he intended—and couldn't wait to feel him against me, deep inside Shaylia's body.

He crowded against her back again, one hand grasping a breast. Rubbing her nipple between his fingers pulled another gasp from Shaylia. "Lean down, Shaylia, so I can make you feel even better."

Her eyelids popped open, and even though arousal widened her pupils, fear slithered in like a venomous snake.

"It's okay, baby," I murmured, rubbing my thumbs in circles on the insides of her thighs. "If you don't want this—"

She leaned down and kissed me, crushing her soft breasts against my chest. "I-I do," she said against my lips. "Just scared it'll hurt."

"If you need him to stop, just say so. He will. Promise."

"I will," Damien agreed and fondled my balls.

I groaned. "Fuck, Damien." I grit my teeth as Shaylia filled herself with my dick and Damien squeezed.

"What's he doing?" Shaylia whispered as she slid forward again, dragging my length along her grasping pussy.

"Squeezing my balls and rimming my ass."

"Oh." His touch left me as she backed fully onto me again, and her eyes widened. "Oh!"

"What's he doing?" I mimicked her question, biting back my smile as she held still.

A small moan slipped past her lips. "He's got his finger in my ass," she whispered, her face flushing red.

"He's getting you ready, baby. Just relax." I tugged her down against me and kissed her, languid with my licks, gently thrusting my tongue between her lips. Every slow nudge of my dick inside her coated my mouth with her moans until she began to rock again.

Damien caressed the back of my dick through the thin membrane of skin between us, and when he added a second finger in Shaylia's ass, she didn't so much as gasp—or stop rocking.

"Oh God," she groaned, lifting her head up and moving back onto my dick and Damien's hand with purpose.

Damien wrapped his other hand in her hair and pulled her upright. My pulse thrummed as he nibbled her throat, her ear, the muscles of his arm disappearing between her thighs, flexing as he finger fucked her ass.

"You're so hot and tight," he growled. "I'm dying to be inside you."

She shuddered, and he released his hold on her. She melted over me again, panting into my neck. "I-I'm ready," she whispered.

Damien groaned, and his fingers disappeared from her ass. I nudged into her soaked pussy twice before she gasped, tensing in my arms.

"Relax, baby," I murmured against her hair, rubbing my hands up and down her back. "Push back against him. Let him in."

I met Damien's gaze as he loomed over us. He held her hips and slowly flexed. The pressure of the head of his dick slipping past her ring of muscles clenched my jaw and ripped a cry from Shaylia.

"Shh," I murmured again, trying to soothe her as Damien gave her time to adjust to the girth of his cock head inside her. My balls ached to explode, but I focused on her. "Relax, baby. Let out a deep breath and let him in."

"Okay," she whispered, shivering in my hold.

I nodded at Damien, and he slid in deeper.

"Oh God, oh God," Shaylia muttered and panted, trembling like crazy, her body tensing fully.

No amount of my soothing hands or murmurings eased the tumbling emotions rolling off her, but the lack of fear, the lack of anxiety kept me from telling Damien to back off.

The pressure of his dick against mine—slowly working his way into her ass, his groans, his words of encouragement on how well she did, how good she felt around his dick—tingled my toes. I didn't move, my balls threatening to erupt.

Damien finally bottomed out with a groan and leaned over Shaylia. "Hey," he whispered, and she turned her head. "You're fucking amazing, Shay." He kissed the corner of her mouth as she moaned and shuddered between us, her eyes clenched shut.

Love rose in my chest, nearly choking me, and my dick jerked inside of her with the need to move.

"Please," Shaylia whispered, trying to writhe between us. "Please … I-I need m-more. Something…"

Damien pulled out, and she groaned deep in her chest. The second he started to push back in, I expelled my held breath and pulled my dick almost fully from her soaked embrace.

She started back up her "Oh God" chant as Damien and I set a rhythm, taking turns fucking into her body with slow, gentle glides.

Damien kissed the words from her lips before kissing me. All three tongues tangled a bit, and the overwhelming surge of emotions, the feeling of *rightness* welled up inside me until I fought off tears.

No annoyance, no anger, no guilt—every negative emotion I'd felt from both in the previous forty-eight hours dissipated from the air.

I'd never felt so complete in my life.

Chapter 23

Shaylia

I came with the force of a hurricane, a rush of cum soaking Ethan as he buried against my womb and groaned his release. Damien thrust twice more inside my ass before letting go, the heat of his cum spurting along with Ethan's, sending another shockwave of climax through me.

My body shook, shivered as a swell of emotion I'd never felt before nearly drowned me. All thought fled, all sense of self dissipated as we came together, the ebbing climax never seeming to end—and ending entirely too soon.

Damien planked over us, his hard chest pressed against my back, the steady thrum of his heart beating in time with Ethan's against my chest.

I panted into Ethan's neck, the softness of his throat against my lips, his whiskers brushing against the bridge of my nose and my clenched eyelids. The clean scent of him, the remnants of Damien's cologne, the muskiness of the mess we'd made filled my lungs.

Heaven, the angel on my shoulder whispered. The devil groaned his agreement.

"Are you okay?" Damien asked—when I'd expected Ethan to be the first to speak.

A shiver rippled me with goosebumps as Damien eased some of his weight off my back, sending a rush of cool air over my heated skin. "Yes," I managed past dry lips.

"Don't move, Shay." Damien smoothed my hair off my shoulder and kissed me on the corner of my mouth. "Be right back."

Ethan wound his arms around me, our hearts thrumming between us.

"So good, Ethan," I murmured into his neck, knowing he already knew how I felt about what we'd done.

He lifted my head and held my face in his hands, his bright green eyes searching mine. "No regrets?"

"Not a single one," I admitted, squeezing my pussy around him.

"Did you agree because you wanted it?"

"Yes." I smiled, needing to ease his conscious.

He heaved a heavy exhale and pulled me close, brushing his lips across mine. We both moaned, and the swell of emotions I'd felt while coming rushed through me again.

"I'm falling in love with you, Shaylia," he murmured, lifting my head again to peer into my eyes. "I know you feel something for me too, but I won't push you. I won't rush this."

"I think we've already gone as far as we can, Ethan." I huffed a shaky laugh.

His smile melted my heart. "You know what I meant."

"I do." I kissed him.

"You two going to give me a show, or can I take care of you?" Damien's voice hinted at laughter—and lust.

I expected one day he'd be sitting in that chair and calling the shots. My pussy twinged at the thought, and I fought the desire to roll my eyes.

Yeah. So much for not allowing anyone control.

I woke to warmth on both sides, a blissful sigh shivering through me. A cracked-open eyelid revealed I faced Damien. He still slept, dark lashes against his tanned cheeks, hair rumpled to perfection, lips parted, his brow relaxed. The lack of consciousness on his face carried youthfulness—I thought he looked familiar in some way.

A shift of his body slid his semi-hard cock against my thigh, and I realized I'd thrown a leg over his hip while we'd slept. I blinked as he opened his eyes, the dark depths of his sleepy orbs sucking all thought from my head.

"Morning, Shay." My name rumbled his chest as he pulled me closer, the sexy curve of his lips heating me through.

I swallowed rather than answer, and he nosed along my jaw, tipping my head back with a nudge.

"You smell so fucking good, like cherries and vanilla," he murmured against my skin, his teeth nipping, and the flex of his ass rubbing his hardened length up along my pussy. "You're wet."

I nodded and gulped.

"Tell me I can have you."

"You can have me."

He slid inside with a mere shift of his hips, and we both moaned.

"Fuck." His arms tightened around me, one hand gripping my ass, one hand tipping my head back to peer into my eyes. Twice, he dragged his length out and slid back in, brushing my womb once buried deep. "I think I like you, Shay."

With one arm trapped between our bodies, I used my other hand to grasp his shoulder. "I like you too, Damien."

"Thank fuck." Ethan's shuddered sigh as he hugged my back shook both Damien and me with laughter.

Our smiles faded as Damien continued to slide in and out of me, holding my gaze with his dark eyes. I wondered at his thoughts, his emotions, but was soon caught up in the need his strokes brought to the edge.

Ethan kissed my neck, my back, his left arm snaking beneath me, between my stomach and Damien's, his other slowly jerking himself against my ass.

"What a way to wake up," he murmured, and I couldn't agree more. He worked his hand lower, brushing over my pubis, two fingers sliding alongside my clit.

"Oh God." I clenched my eyes shut and bucked, suddenly needing more than unhurried, slow thrusts from Damien.

Ethan groaned, resting his forehead against the back of my head, fisting himself a bit faster against my back while gently rubbing my clit.

"Please." I licked my lower lip, my hips undulating, chasing after what I wanted.

"Do you want to come, Shay?" Damien's rumbled voice sent a rush of wetness around his thrusting cock.

"Yes. Please, yes."

"Ethan," he said, his word a command.

Ethan rubbed me faster, and Damien thrust in deep with a grunt, pulled out, and thrust hard again.

"Oh God!" I swallowed a gasp, and my climax exploded. "God!" I shrieked, my pussy clamping down on Damien.

He worked me hard and fast, hitting my womb, and drawing every last spasm from my soaked core.

As one, he and Ethan groaned, cum coating my lower back and inside my pussy.

Gasping for breath, we finally stilled. A shuddering sigh rippled through me, and I opened my eyes.

Damien peered at me a brief moment before brushing his lips over mine.

I wished for Ethan's ability to feel emotion, so I might know Damien's toward me. Same as the night before, he crawled from bed first to retrieve towels for me and Ethan, and I stared at the ripple of muscle in his back and ass as he walked away, his cum dripping from my body.

Ethan kissed the back of my head and sighed. "Thank you."

"For?" I asked, reaching my hand back to caress from his hip to his powerful thigh.

"For making me the happiest man on earth."

Joy filled me, and I wanted to wallow in warmth and smiles. Doing so had made me happy too—and not just for pleasing him. I eyed Damien returning with wet towels for us, and my heart did a little fluttered dance.

"So happy, Shaylia," Ethan murmured against my hair and sighed again.

Chapter 24

Ethan

For the first time in my life, I felt as though I'd been dealt a new hand of cards, one I could work with, one that would run in my favor. I couldn't contain my grin while heading into the gallery.

I'd left the place closed on Saturday since I'd been too overwhelmed between the confrontation with Shaylia and her coming to dinner that night. I hated to leave my two lovers on our first full day together, but they needed time to bond—without me between them.

Whistling, I unlocked the gallery and flicked on the lights, my heart near to bursting. Memories of Shaylia writhing between us, the rightness of how the three of us came together hardened me a few times during the remainder of the morning, but I wasn't about to waste the load brewing in my balls.

A handful of customers strode into the shop before noon, and whether my happiness boosted their own—which it did—or they truly loved my work, two couples walked out with wrapped paintings.

My spirits soared.

The mail arrived, and I saved a square envelope for last since it showed no evidence of being a bill and neat script penned my name.

I finally tore it open, and my breath caught as two personal invitations to the art show I'd begged Damien to attend with me fell out. My throat thickened as I realized it must be his doing. I'd mentioned the show to Shaylia and how bummed I'd been about not being able to get tickets, but I doubted she had the connections to get what I held in my hand.

Not just tickets but personal invites, the type that would be printed for family and close friends of Jack and Trevor, the world's hottest artists who'd risen to world-wide fame shortly before their *Perfection* painting was released to the world five years earlier.

I grabbed my phone. "Hey," I said the second Damien answered. "Did you get these tickets?"

He chuckled. "I told you there wasn't anything I wouldn't do."

I swallowed against the thickness in my throat, threatening to choke off my words. "That was the most thoughtful thing you've ever done for me, Damien."

"I should have spoiled you like this the past fifteen years." His low tone hinted at guilt.

I wanted to tell him I loved him but didn't wish to feel the disappointment of not hearing it in return. "Thank you."

"Wish I could do more to make it up to you."

"Any chance you could get a third for Shaylia?" I asked with a laugh, not really meaning it.

"Shouldn't be a problem. My cousin can hook me up."

"You're the best, Damien."

"And don't you forget it."

A horn sounded in the background. "Still on the Duck Tour?" I asked since they'd planned on that as part of their sight-seeing Boston when I'd left for the gallery.

"Finished up a bit ago. Going to grab a shrimp scampi pizza at Ernesto's."

"I'm jealous." My mouth watered.

"You should be." Damien laughed, sounding more relaxed than I'd heard in a long time. "I've got a gorgeous woman with me, and she's blushing as we speak."

"Lucky bastard."

"Got that right." I could imagine his grin. "I'll get a pizza to go too."

"You're the best," I said again, my own smile stretching my mouth.

We hung up a few seconds later, and even though I missed him and Shaylia to the point my chest ached, hope for our future kept me on cloud nine in their absence.

Chapter 25

Damien

I stared at Shaylia licking a bit of sauce from the corner of her lip, the lazy slide of her tongue twitching my dick in my jeans for at least the tenth time since we'd left the condo that morning.

We'd taken a slow, meandering walk along the harbor before the duck tour, chatting, even holding hands briefly after she stumbled once. She turned out to be as agreeable and sweet as Ethan had claimed, and even though I didn't have the comfort of her feeling my emotions as he did, I found it easier than I'd expected to open up a bit to her.

"You're staring again." She laughed, reaching for her sweating bottle of Sam Adams.

"Can't help it." I grinned, lifting my focus to her twinkling blue eyes. "You're hot. Sexy." I leaned forward on the small tabletop between us, holding her gaze as her cheeks flushed again. "And I actually like you."

One of her eyebrows shot up. "Meaning, you didn't expect to?"

"I don't like too many people, and with you holding a part of Ethan's heart…"

Her smile faded, as did mine. "Tell me how you met."

"What all did Ethan already tell you?"

"Doesn't matter," she said, picking up her slice of pizza again. "I want to hear about it from your perspective."

"We were roommates our freshman year in college. We liked each other, were both horny fuckers, and he ended up feeding my desire to dominate someone."

A shiver slid over her when I used the word "dominate."

"Were you always bi?" she asked a bit breathless.

"Didn't know it until the first time I saw him, the lost look in his hazel-green eyes like he needed someone to protect him from the world. When I found out *why* that look filled his face, I felt like I'd found my calling, the reason for my life."

"So, what happened next?" Her smile twitched my dick.

While I didn't open up with anyone but Ethan—and it often came to teeth pulling, at that—I found myself wanting Shaylia to know me. I wanted our relationship to grow into something promising. I actually held hope it would, even though I would keep up a wall of sorts to protect us in the event she proved to be a wily, money-hungry bitch.

"My stepfather ran my grandfather's company into the ground through some illegal dealings," I mentioned again what I'd briefly touched on the night before.

She frowned while sipping her beer. "Ethan mentioned your mother almost had to declare bankruptcy."

"Yep." The old familiar anger thinking about the entire fucked-up embezzlement situation sizzled to life in my stomach, denting my brow. "He ruined my family name, but that was a long time ago, and now, the business is prospering."

Shaylia studied my face for a few moments as though trying to figure something out in her own mind. "Did you ever forgive him?"

"Fuck, no," I didn't hesitate to answer. "Still hurts," I admitted. "Still makes me angry. The man my mom allowed in our lives, the man I'd grown to love like the father I'd never known betrayed us."

She nodded, her eyes welling. "My dad left us when I was eight, so I understand betrayal all-too well."

"I'm sorry," I said the same as I had over dinner and reached across the table to grab her hand, needing the physical connection, something I'd never felt before.

Her attempted smile wobbled as she squeezed my fingers. "I never forgave him either. Knowing I wasn't good enough for him has driven me in life. While I don't have the brain to be a surgeon or a lawyer, I've striven to be the best me I can be—even if it is only a secretary."

"I think you're pretty kick-ass," I murmured, smiling. "And Madeline has been dropping hints about our needing to hire you full-time."

Shaylia blinked. "Really?"

"Yep. She says you're a breath of fresh air, a hard worker, a *good* worker."

The hurt disappeared from her face, and her slow smile flipped my stomach in a way I hadn't experienced since first seeing Ethan. "She said I was a good worker?"

I nodded. "You're happier your co-worker offered a compliment over mine about you being sexy?"

"I liked your compliment, too." She laughed, her eyes twinkling again.

"What do you say we box the rest of our pizza up and head home?"

Gaze narrowing but still smiling, she tilted her head. "Got something on your mind, Damien?"

"Yeah, but it's not where *your* mind is going."

"Oh?"

"I'm in the mood to bake some cookies."

"What?" She laughed again while sitting back.

"Cookies. Ethan loves homemade chocolate chip cookies like his nanny used to make."

"Have you made them before?"

I stood to retrieve the takeout box and pizza I'd ordered for Ethan. "Nope, but I know where he keeps the recipe. Figured between the pizza and cookies, he'll owe us big time."

"Oh." Pink tinged her cheeks again. "Well then, let's go."

Chapter 26

Shaylia

Damien felt me up while I tried to spoon out the tablespoons of cookie dough onto sheets that looked like they'd never been used. He held my breasts in both hands, rubbing my straining nipples between his fingers. Even though my bra and shirt separated our skin, his touch seared me and sent waves of arousal straight to my clit.

He nuzzled my neck. "Vanilla never smelled so good."

I giggled and pulled away to put the pan in the oven. The second the oven door shut, Damien spun me and grabbed my hands.

My breath caught as he sucked one of my fingers into his warm, wet mouth, flicks of his tongue cleaning me of smeared batter. Wetness seeped from me, dampening my panties. Until he finished cleaning my other finger, my pussy pulsed along with the blood in my arteries.

He held me captive with his dark eyes, filled with a lust I couldn't ignore. "I want you," he murmured, his hands sliding down to grasp my ass and pull me tight against his hard body.

I licked my lower lip, my body on board, my head questioning. "What about Ethan?"

"What about him?" He ground his hips, rubbing his hard cock against my lower abdomen.

"Shouldn't we wait for him?" My voice came out breathless with need.

"He wanted us to connect today." Damien's focus slipped to my mouth. My neck. "*Bond.*" A smirk curled his mouth as he ensnared my gaze again. "I'm sure he's expecting us to fuck."

The way he half-growled the last word weakened my knees, and I knew I wouldn't be able to say no even if I'd wanted to. The man oozed sexual aggression in a

way I never thought I would like, magnetism I couldn't
—didn't—want to ignore.

Damien leaned down and kissed me, his mouth
possessive, his tongue hot and demanding.

I whimpered and yanked him closer. My mind emptied.
Sagging against him, I wound my hands around his
neck as his fingers dug into my ass, lifting me. Settled
around his waist, I clung to Damien as he strode
toward the bedroom.

Setting me on my feet, he stepped back, rubbing the
hard length trapped in his jeans along his right thigh.

"Take off your clothes and lie on the bed."

My hands shook—from nervousness and need alike—
but I did as told, my lower lip between my teeth as first
my panties, then my bra landed soundlessly on the
floor. Wetness coated my thighs, and my puckered
nipples ached for his mouth.

"You're beautiful, Shay," he said, his tone low and
strangled.

I barely refrained from snorting, but he caught my
gaze, his brow raised. "What? You don't believe me?"

A shrug lifted my shoulder since vocalizing what I thought about my out-of-shape body with its big boobs would kill the sexual tension zapping between us.

"You're absolutely perfect, and if I ever hear you say anything otherwise,"—Damien's gaze narrowed—"I'll redden your ass. Got it?"

I gulped as my pussy spasmed at the thought of him bending me over his lap and slapping my ass. The thought of violence, even in a sexual sense, had never turned me on, but the thought of Damien punishing me, marking me with his hands heated me through.

"Your chest is flushing." A cocky smile lifted the corner of his lip as he moved closer. "You must want my hand print on you."

"I-I don't know."

He huffed a laugh and pressed his index finger between my breasts. "Lie down, Shay."

I sat on the bed's edge and started to scoot back, but he grasped my hips and kept me on the bed's edge.

"Feet up," he murmured, spreading me wide, his stare on my pussy trickling wetness from me. He groaned and knelt between my thighs as I planted my heels on the mattress. "So pretty," he murmured, spreading my labia with his thumbs. "So pink and juicy."

The first swipe of his tongue up over my hole and clit bowed my back off the bed, and I gasped, grasping hold of his head. "Oh God..." I moaned as he licked again, a single finger sliding deep inside me as he latched onto my clit.

"Not going to last, Damien," I managed to gasp as he pumped his finger inside me, his teeth gently nibbling on my throbbing clit. He took me to the edge and backed off, leaving me panting, dripping.

I propped up on my elbows as he stripped, revealing every glorious inch of his hard, muscled body. Pecs I wanted to sink my teeth into overlooked a ripple of abdominal muscles, and the cock jutting up, its slit leaking turned on my mouth's water works. Swallowing, I lifted my attention to his face. "I-I want to taste you too."

He held out a hand, and I took it. Pulled upright, I stared at the hard cock in front of my face. His other hand wrapped around the base, holding it toward me in offering.

I slid my hand down his length before closing my mouth over the slickened head and grasping his balls.

He groaned and fisted both hands in my hair, tugging me closer until he bottomed out against the back of my throat. "How much can you take, Shay?" he asked, his voice wrecked as he pulled out of my mouth.

"I want it all," I said, flicking my tongue across his slit.

With another groan, he sank back in, and I relaxed my throat, determined to nuzzle my nose against his groin as I'd seen Ethan do. He bottomed out, and his curses and the twitch of his cock deep in my throat pleased me enough, I smiled around his girth.

"Fuck, Shay." He pulled me off him with a pop and pushed me down on the bed, climbing over me, the hunger in his eyes like that of a starved lion.

He claimed my mouth and slid deep inside my pussy. A rush swept through me—arousal, need, pure exquisite emotion—and I lost my breath.

Slow and easy, he made love to me, dragging his length along my clasping walls, pushing back in to seat against my cervix. His groans in my mouth as he fucked mine with his tongue shivered my skin. Lifting my hips to meet him wasn't enough, I needed to be closer—inside his soul, the same as I felt with Ethan every time we made love.

"Need," I whispered against his mouth as he tugged on my lower lip with his teeth.

"I know, baby," he murmured, sliding one arm beneath my leg and lifting my knee close to my ear. "I know."

Opened fully, pinned to the mattress, I clutched at his dampening back, finding purchase to cling to as he flexed his ass and ground his pelvis against me. Faster. Harder.

"Oh." I clenched my eyes shut as my climax drew near.

"Look at me."

My eyelids popped open in obedience, and I panted, desperately wanting the tingles growing in my toes to erupt throughout my entire body.

Damien angled his hips and drove into me with such force, I shrieked—and came around his cock.

"Yes, Shay," he growled and thrust again, harder, arching my back. "Give it all to me—yes."

I dug my fingernails into his back and cried out again.

He wrapped his arms around me with a deep groan, and slammed into me over and over, drawing out my climax. A heaved grunt, and his cum shot deep inside me. "So good." He thrust. "So fucking good."

One last thrust and he stilled, holding his weight from smooshing me into the bed. Sweat slickened between us, our hearts pounding, our breaths rapid. My muscles grew lax as I rubbed my palms up and down his spine, squeezing his softening length with my pussy.

He groaned and lifted his head, kissing me deeply.

The scent of burning wafted past my nose, and I realized the oven's timer dinged from the kitchen.

"Shit!" I pushed at Damien, and the fire alarm went off. Giggling and leaking cum down my legs, I hurried into the kitchen.

Smoke poured from the oven, and still laughing, I grabbed the oven mitt, yanked the door open, and pulled out the burned cookies.

Damien grumbled behind me, and I bit my lip as he shoved a few windows open before grabbing a hand towel to waft beneath the smoke detector.

The damn thing finally quieted, and I caught his gaze.

Laughter erupted from both of us.

I'd burned the last tray of cookies, but it had been worth it. Rumpled hair atop his head, his eyes sated of hunger, his cock drooping and glistening…

"Shower?" I suggested, still smiling.

He tossed the towel onto the counter, atop the blackened cookies and scooped me up into his arms. The mess between my thighs smeared over his arm, and I shifted, trying to keep from getting it all over him.

"Hold still."

"But I'm leaking cum all over your arm."

"Don't care." He brushed his lips over mine as he kicked the bathroom door shut behind us. "I've never been so happy to be a sticky mess."

"That a fact?" I asked, a soft smile on my lips as I ran my fingers through his hair.

"Mmm." He set me on my feet and reached to turn on the shower. "And I can't wait for tonight when it'll be all three of us making that mess."

Even though he'd ripped one hell of an orgasm out of me, my pussy tightened again at the thought of having them both. I'd felt so content with Ethan—as though I'd found a missing part of my life—but with Damien's introduction into said life, I realized I'd been missing out on so much more.

See? Three can work, my devil mused with a sigh.

I climbed into the shower, and Damien wrapped his arms around me again, pulling me back into the spray.

Sunday was a day of rest for us, but the following morning would be a true test. How would things be at work? Both men in their offices, me in the reception area with Madeline… Would I manage to keep my feelings in check? Hide my emotions toward the two men who had swept me off my feet?

What if their other employees caught wind of our affair? I expected they would all believe I fucked them in the hope of getting hired full-time or taking Madeline's job when she retired in a few months.

The high of my climax and the happiness of the weekend dimmed a bit as questions continued to swarm my head.

Perhaps three might not *work,* the angel on my shoulder whispered my fear.

Chapter 27

Damien

I sat back in my office chair, gazing out over Boston. Rain slashed at the windows and had kept me from my normal morning run, but I didn't give a shit. Staying in bed until the last possible minute with Ethan had been worth it.

Shaylia had spent most of Sunday evening with us, but that morning, I wanted my man … and I had him—face down on the mattress, my dick so far up his ass, he whimpered with every thrust. Lying like that kept him from jerking off, but I'd made it up to him, allowing him to blow his load down my throat once I'd finished. He'd been full of sighs and thank yous, running his hands through my hair as though petting me for being such a good boy.

I'd promised he could make it up to me later.

I eyed the clock. Only noon.

I'd called a meeting with my two lovers for one when Madeline went to lunch, and my dick ached at the thought of locking the doors and taking what I wanted.

While I wasn't a Dom who needed to inflict pain, I sure as hell enjoyed my two lovers' submission to my commands in bed.

I shifted on my chair and dropped my hand to my lap to work my stiff dick inside my slacks, clearing my desk with the other. I'd need a bit of room for what I had planned—a quickie with Shaylia bent over the edge of my desk, Ethan's dick in her pussy while she sucked my cock.

Not for an hour, I thought, glancing at my computer's clock in the corner—again.

Heaving a heavy exhale, I pulled my chair closer, but still palmed my dick. Two files sat beside me, both which needed signing off, but they could wait. Three email notifications had dinged in the last hour, so I clicked on the icon, pulling them up.

My cell rang and seeing "Mom" on the screen, I picked up, rather than ignore like I usually did during office hours.

"Mom," I said, sitting back in my chair again. "Everything okay?"

"They're releasing him."

The meaning escaped me as I worked through the anger lacing her words. "What?"

"He who shall not be fucking named is getting released from jail this weekend."

I blinked at my mother's use of profanity—and the realization of what she'd meant. "How the fuck?"

"I don't know," she all but growled. "Probably good behavior or some such shit."

"Mom."

"I can curse if I want! He's a lying douchebag who can manipulate like no other!" She huffed a breath, and even though the thought of my ex-stepfather getting out of jail pissed me the hell off, I couldn't help but be amused by my mother's fire. He'd been the first to bring it out of her, and any mention of him—named or not named—set her off.

"It's been a long time," I said, hoping to calm her down. "Like you, I'll never forgive him, but we have to try to leave the past where it belongs."

She huffed again but didn't comment.

"Think about where our company is now, Mom. Where Ethan has helped take us."

"You're right," she said with a sigh. "How is that sweet boy?"

"Sweet as ever," I said with a smile, hating my heart didn't swell back to what it had been before her call. "I've got some news, by the way."

Might as well drop the bomb.

"You're finally going to marry him?"

"No," I snorted.

"You need to make an honest man out of Ethan, Damien."

I shifted on my chair at the tone that used to curl my toes when I'd done something wrong. "We ... ah, met someone."

Mom didn't reply right away, so I waited, giving her time to process. "Meaning?" she asked after a few seconds.

"Meaning..." I said, drawing the word out. "There's a young woman we're both seeing."

Her silence twisted my stomach.

"I know it's not the norm," I said, hoping to ease her, rather than get her panties in yet a deeper twist, "but we both really like her, and so far, it seems to be going rather well."

"How is Ethan handling a double dose of emotions?"

My mother knew Ethan almost as well as I did and had always had a soft spot in her heart for him. He'd often come to our house when overrun from humanity's emotions battling against him.

"Surprisingly well."

I filled Mom in a bit on the budding relationship with the three of us, and before hanging up, she offered her best wishes—and begged me to remain as cool as I sounded over the phone.

I hung up, knowing why she worried. The mere mention of that asshole who nearly ruined us usually got me riled to the point, I enjoyed more than a fair share of Grey Goose. Sometimes, I got angry enough to start a fight with whatever asshole sat or stood close enough and looked at me wrong.

While anger and bitterness stewed in my stomach, I didn't feel the need to punch anyone—or a wall.

Memories crashed against me, twisting my insides anew. I had given that man my love, the top-most spot on the pedestal of those I admired when I was a kid, and he'd betrayed, not just me, but the only woman I'd ever loved.

Mom would never forgive him, same as me, and while over the years, therapists had encouraged looking toward our future rather than the past, the news of his release brought it all back with force.

I remembered all over again why I didn't trust anyone but Ethan. I remembered why I shielded my heart and my mind from the manipulation of others. The broken heart of a seventeen-year-old kid still beat in my chest, but the years had hardened me toward the hurt.

While Shaylia had managed to ease past my walls a bit, I grimaced at the thought of being completely vulnerable ever again. For Ethan, I would continue on our path with her. For Ethan, I would accept her in our lives.

But I would *never* trust her.

Ethan poked his head through the door separating our offices. "Meeting time?" he asked, his eyes twinkling.

Still scowling, I clicked open the first of my emails— and found an excuse to cancel.

"I've got too much going on," I muttered, not meeting his gaze, glancing through my London manager's email. "Why don't you and Shaylia go out for lunch? I'll catch you all later tonight."

"Oh." Disappointment coated the single word, and I wondered if he would ask about the anger he must feel radiating off me. "Are you okay?" he asked, exactly as I'd expected.

"Yeah." Forcing a smile, I turned toward him. "Just got some shit to deal with in the London office. I'll be fine."

"Need to talk?"

"Not now," I said, returning to my computer, "but thanks."

He shut the door without another word, and I blew a breath between my lips. I was a lying sack of shit, but Ethan didn't need to bear my burden. Determined to simmer down by the end of the day, I picked up the phone to call the other office and calm the London manager's jets.

Doing so took my mind off the news and the wondering over the future for the three of us. Without trust, I knew a long-term relationship wouldn't work. Maybe I would get lucky, and Shaylia would call it quits long before I ended up ruining what they both seemed to think was something pretty special.

You do, too.

I scowled at the words whispered in my head and shot them down with the sharp reminder of why I couldn't allow someone control over my heart—ever again.

Chapter 28

Ethan

Saturday morning, Shaylia decided to tag along with me to the gallery, and while I loved to be with her, I'd almost insisted she stay with Damien to see if she could break through his funk and get him to talk.

The night before, he didn't get home from work until nine, and he'd been closed-mouthed more than usual. Once showered, he'd crawled into bed—and for the first time in a week, he didn't fuck either one of us. Muttering about exhaustion from the long day, dealing with the London office drama, he'd fallen asleep within a half hour.

I wondered at the anger that laid beneath his words, and while it certainly wasn't directed at either of us, I recognized his closing us out as easily as a door shut in my face. Shaylia, at least, didn't seem to catch onto Damien's mood, and we'd cuddled and kissed, whispering long after Damien slept.

He'd been up and outside running with the sunrise, and we left not long after he returned and hopped in the shower. At least we both got a quick smooch from his heated lips. The clean scent of his sweat darkening and plastering his hair to his head had sent a wave of need through me even though we'd had sex a record number of times since Shaylia had agreed to share our bed.

"So, next week you're part time," Shaylia said, handing me a cup of coffee in the gallery's back room.

I sat at one of the two chairs beside the tiny table I'd bought from IKEA and patted my lap. The chair beneath us squeaked when she settled her weight on my thigh, and I grabbed her waist to keep her in place when she attempted to jump up with a gasp.

"This chair—"

"Will be fine," I assured her, wiggling my ass to prove my point. The piece of metal remained intact, unbothered by our combined weight.

She smiled and cupped my cheek. "You've done an amazing job with the gallery, Ethan."

Her edification swelled my heart, and I couldn't help beaming at her with all the love and thankfulness I felt growing inside me. "It's all because of you, you know."

"Bull." She laughed lightly before brushing her lips over mine. "You planned on doing this even before I started working for you."

"Yes." I slid my hand down over the top of her rounded ass and squeezed the flesh propped on my thigh. "But having your encouragement made doing so that much easier. Made it a joy when it would have been bittersweet."

"Damien seems to be happy for you."

"He is,"—my brow furrowed for a second, but I smoothed it out, not wanting to worry her—"but the true revealing of his feelings will happen next week when I'm only at his beck-and-call in the office two days rather than five."

"He'll survive."

I set my coffee aside and cradled her face in my hands, soaking in her happiness, her openness to showing me affection. "Knowing you're there to soothe him will make it easier for me."

"Soothe him?" One of her brows rose along with the corner of her lips. "Hmm." A glint lit her blue eyes. "I could think of a few ways I might do that, but it would hardly be proper with him being my boss."

My dick twitched at the thought of her on her knees, sucking him off in in his office like I'd done dozens of times. "Just lock the door," I said, my voice low. "You'll be safe and sound. Promise."

"You say that as though you know from experience."

"He keeps a bottle of lube in his bottom drawer," I said as my dick swelled, strangling in my jeans.

"Oh?" Her eyebrow popped up again, and she bit on her lower lip.

I leaned forward and nipped her ear. "He likes to bend me over his desk when his blood pressure gets too high, and he needs to let off steam. He lands a few swats on me sometimes, and I'm sure he'd gladly do the same to you if you bared your ass."

"Damn," she whispered.

"Are you getting wet, Shaylia?" I asked, breathing against her ear.

"Yes."

"Think this table can handle my bending you over it?

"Ethan." She breathed my name, but the damn bell over the door tinkled, letting me know someone had entered.

I stood and set her aside, hesitant to do so even though a potential buyer stood in the next room. "We'll pick up this conversation in a bit." A quick peck and I hurried out to see who'd come in.

* * *

I made a sale, and grinning ear to ear, I swooped Shaylia into my arms once they left, kissing her firmly on the lips.

"Did you hear him say he's going to let his 'art-whore friends' know about the gallery?"

"I heard." Pure happiness radiated on her face—and off her body when I put her down again.

"God, you make me happy." I grabbed her waist and pulled her close to kiss her again. "Thank you for this," I said with a sigh against her lips. "Thank you for being open to Damien too. He had a great time with you last weekend."

"It was kind of nice having him alone." Shaylia pulled away and headed to the back room, and I tracked after her, my gaze on her ass.

"We ought to take turns dating you every week."

"I'm up for that," she murmured, her eyes twinkling when she turned and leaned against the counter.

"I'm up for you." I palmed myself through my jeans, and her focus dropped to my hand.

"So, I see." Her tongue flitted out to swipe her lower lip, leaving a wet sheen behind. "Perhaps, you should go lock the door." She unsnapped her jeans and shoved them to her knees, along with her panties.

I groaned as my dick jerked in my hand.

"Hurry," she whispered, leaning over the small table, her round ass and pussy lips salivating my mouth.

I obeyed without hesitation, and we celebrated my sale in the best way possible. Luckily, the table survived.

Chapter 29

Damien

My run had gotten me out of my head and lessened my anger. Until Ethan and Shaylia came back to the condo Saturday afternoon, I didn't worry about Ethan picking up on any negative feelings from me. Determination to keep from being too vulnerable to Shaylia, however, remained firmly rooted in my stubborn head.

Although I enjoyed her company, I wasn't upset she decided to go home that night. Ethan and I laid in bed, his head on my chest as I ran my fingers through his thick hair.

"Are you happy?" he asked, his voice low, uncertain.

I thought about *his* happiness with the gallery. "I am."

"Something is bothering you, though."

I considered my feelings, my thoughts, but discussing either regarding our relationship wouldn't keep his happiness in place.

"My ex-stepdad was released on Friday." I went with that truth instead since the news still bothered the fuck out of me.

Ethan sat up, his brow furrowed as he stared down at me in the bedroom's dimmed light. "Why didn't you tell me?"

"I didn't want to upset you." I tried for a smile. "You've been on cloud nine lately, and I'd hate to see anything put you in a funk."

Ethan continued to study me, and I wondered at the emotions beneath my thoughts and what he might believe of them. "He can't hurt you anymore."

"I know that, but the betrayal still hurts."

"You'll never be able to forgive him, will you?"

"No."

"If you don't at least try to let your anger go,"—Ethan exhaled heavily—"it will fester."

"I've tried, Ethan." I frowned. "It's fucking impossible."

He took my hand, placing our palms together before entwining our fingers and squeezing. "I'll always be here if you need to talk."

I tugged him toward me and brushed my lips over his, trying to show him what I felt, that all I desired was his happiness.

* * *

Monday morning madness ruled the damn office. One of our top advisors quit without notice, and I scrambled to incorporate his clientele into my schedule until we could find a replacement for his ass.

Head pounding, I slugged down a third cup of coffee, knowing a late night at the office was before me. At least the London drama had simmered down. I needed to head back over the pond before too long though and get everything set up properly.

Madeline buzzed me on the intercom.

"Yes?" I asked, distracted by an email from the London manager.

"Dee Miller is here to see you."

My mind blanked for a moment before her words sank in. Dee Miller ... the man who almost ruined my family's name. "I'm sorry?" I asked to be doubly sure, my voice suddenly ragged.

"Dee Miller." Disgust laced Madeline's voice. She knew who he was, what he'd done since she had worked for my grandfather when the shit went down.

What the fuck? I scrubbed a hand down over my face. I had no fucking clue what he could want from me.

A job? I snorted. "As fucking if," I muttered.

To ask forgiveness? "No fucking way."

I hit the intercom button. "You can send him in, Madeline."

I stood and straightened my tie and jacket, but made no move to round my desk to greet him.

The door opened, and a mere shell of the man I'd known entered, a too-big suit hanging off his stooped shoulders. Where a pile of dark hair used to crown his head, mere wisps of white revealed the spotted scalp beneath.

He met my gaze for less than a heartbeat before focusing on the floor. "Damien. I was sorry to hear about your grandfather."

I kept silent as the door shut behind him, my scowl firmly set. He could say he was sorry for all kinds of shit, but that wouldn't change things between us. My grandfather had passed in his sleep, never having forgiven Dee for what he'd done, and neither would I.

Dee glanced up again quickly, taking in my bearing—my attire. "You look well."

"You don't," I snipped, uncaring of the cringe my truthful observation caused on his face.

"I have pancreatic cancer. It's terminal."

Shit. The fight actually went out of me as I realized what I had wished for years would come true, sooner than later. I would never forgive Dee, but I couldn't toss him out on his ass like I wanted to. I motioned toward the chair across from me and sat, reaching for the intercom button again.

"Madeline, send in some coffee, please."

"Yes, sir." She didn't sound pleased, and while I wasn't either, I refused to be an absolute asshole to a dying man—no matter who he was.

Chapter 30

Shaylia

Ethan and I snuck back to the office after a quick lunch. Damien hadn't been able to go with us, so we brought back a steak tip salad with extra blue cheese for him. While I'd have rather held Ethan's hand or snuggled against his side while entering the office, I stepped away, needing to keep the proper distance.

Warmth still spread through me from the whispers we'd shared over our lunches, the promise of what our night might hold since I'd already agreed to spend my evening with the two men.

Sure my face was still flushed, I kept my head down when the elevator door opened, and we stepped into the reception area.

"Oh, good, you're back." Madeline's statement lifted my head. "Would you mind taking coffee into Damien," she asked, standing and grabbing her purse from her desk, her lips pressed tight.

"Sure," I agreed, excitement over finally getting a peek at my other boss coursing through me.

"I'll warn you," Madeline said, pulling my wandering focus off Ethan's ass as he approached his own office door. "He's in a meeting, and he's not happy."

"Who is it?" I glanced at Damien's shut door.

"That asshole of a stepfather," she snipped as though well acquainted with the man.

Ethan pulled up short and glanced her way, his brow furrowed.

"What does *he* want?" Ethan asked at the same time I tossed out a question wondering what he was doing in the office.

"Darned if I know." Madeline rounded her desk and started toward the elevators. "I'm off to lunch. Thanks for taking the coffee. If I had to lay eyes on *that man* one more time, I just might spit."

Ethan scowled at Damien's door, working his lower lip as Madeline strode off, leaving us alone.

"Can you feel anything?" I asked, keeping my voice low.

"Not a goddamn thing."

I tried to not wring my hands as my lunch churned in my stomach. Damien hadn't shared much with me about the man who had almost ruined him and his mother, but I knew it wouldn't be a pleasant atmosphere behind the door.

"What should I do?" I whispered, glancing once more at Ethan.

"Take them coffee," he said. "If Damien requested beverages, it can't be too bad even though I find that hard as hell to imagine."

I hurried to the counter behind Madeline's desk and popped a K-cup into the Keurig as Ethan disappeared into his office. The excitement of seeing Damien had dissolved into gut-wrenching nervousness. Things had been going so smoothly among the three of us, I'd actually held hope we might evolve into a steady relationship.

With Damien upset, I knew Ethan would be as well. Perhaps it would be best if I didn't spend the night but gave the two men time to discuss and work out whatever emotions the man with Damien stirred up.

Heaving a heavy sigh, I picked up the small tray and tapped on Damien's door.

"Enter!" he barked.

Great. Pissy.

Forcing a smile Ethan at least would discern as fake, I pushed the door in.

Thin graying hair topped Damien's guest, who sat with his back toward me. I glanced at Damien, but he stared at his visitor, his dark eyes steel and fire.

"You can put it here on the desk," he told me, his tone bland as he motioned to his right.

I approached, and the man turned when I came alongside him, his blue-eyed gaze crashing against my face.

Blue as the sky—the same as mine.

My breath caught, and I stumbled, the tray sliding from my suddenly numb hands, crashing to the wooden floor. "What…"

Blinking, I turned to Damien, and the memory of his youthful face in sleep wavered through my brain.

No.

He rose to his feet, his brow furrowing. "Shaylia?"

A shudder rippled through me, shaking me from head to toe. "No, no, no…" My voice came out as a ragged whisper, but Damien stared, frowning—I turned back to the old man.

My pulse thrummed but in the worst way possible.

"Shaylia…" The rushing blood in my ears hushed the old man's voice as he said my name.

"You know one another?" Damien asked, his voice hard as he appeared in my periphery vision.

As I stared at the sunken form of the man I used to know, Ethan's door opened, but I couldn't look away from the blue eyes I'd inherited.

I swallowed back a sob and barely managed to whisper, "He's my father."

Chapter 31

Ethan

I pulled up short in the opened doorway as Shaylia's hurt slammed into me with enough force to steal my breath. Blinking, I scanned the office's three occupants, sure I hadn't heard Shaylia's declaration right.

Damien's scowl deepened, and the potent anger radiating off him stood the hairs on my arms on end.

Shaylia sobbed and slapped a hand over her mouth before spinning and stumbling from the office.

"What the fuck?" Damien half-shouted. "Goddamnit!" He turned a murderous glare on Dee. "Take your goddamn apologies and get the fuck out!"

I found my feet and rushed after Shaylia. She poked at the elevator button, her keening cries and swallows tearing at my heart.

"Shaylia!" I called. "Wait! Please!"

Without looking at me, she spun toward the stairwell and slammed the metal door open.

"Shit." I ran and grabbed the door to keep from sliding past. "Shaylia!"

Her heels clacked on the stairs, her sobs echoing up the stairwell.

I leaped down stairs, catching her before descending two floors. "Shaylia," I whispered, grabbing her arm and spinning her toward me.

She allowed me to pull her close, and my vision hazed at the level of hurt and sadness pouring off her. I had no words, zero thoughts on how to offer comfort other than with my arms.

"Ruined," she finally managed through her tears, her voice muffled against my chest.

I smoothed my hands up and down her back, my cheek pressed to the top of her head.

"Why?" She sniffed and pulled back a few inches, peering up at me through her tears. "Why did it have to be him? Why?" More tears poured down her cheeks as I cradled her face in my hands, lowering my face to meet hers.

She stared at me as though begging for an answer I didn't have. I wish I could have claimed I didn't understand her hurt over finding out her lover was actually the young man she'd always weighed herself against.

The boy who had stolen her father from her.

What a fucked-up situation. I worked my lower lip, wracking my brain but came up empty. "Let me take you home."

Shaylia jerked her head up and down, and I squeezed her arms.

"I have to go grab my keys. Can you stay here? Please?"

"Yes," she whispered, swiping wetness from her cheeks. "Can you get my purse from beneath my desk?"

I nodded and sprinted back up the stairs. The elevator dinged, the numbers plunging down when I stepped into the hallway.

Damien stood in his office door, his gaze murderous. "Dee said he didn't send her here, but he's full of shit! I know he sent that bitch to take us down!"

I stalked forward and got in his face. "Calm the fuck down before you make a scene, Damien," I growled, his anger raising my own. "I *know* Shaylia wasn't sent here by him. The level of hurt she's experiencing..." I winced, her grief consuming my own misery.

"You're sure?" he asked, his gaze hard as flint, tension radiating off him.

"Absolutely." I nodded. "Shut yourself in your office. Have a shot or two to take the edge off, and let me take care of this mess, okay?"

A muscle jumped in his jaw as he stared at me.

"Please," I whispered, laying my hand on his chest.

He blinked twice before stepping back, his eyes still hard, but his voice level. "I trust you, Ethan, but this goes beyond something you can fix. She's Dee's fucking daughter!" Damien turned and slammed his door behind him.

I swallowed against the ache knifing my chest. The previous couple of weeks had given me so much happiness, so much joy—and within a single moment, I found myself floundering, torn apart from the inside by a cruel twist of fate.

Jaw clenched, I hurried into my office and grabbed my keys before returning for Shaylia's purse. I found her where I'd left her, her arms wrapped around her center as she leaned against the cement wall, head tipped back and eyes closed. Wetness continued to seep from her eyelids, tracking down her cheeks.

My heart beat heavily, and my mind swamped with emotions I had no control over. Grasping her elbow, I tugged her against my side. "Come on."

She stumbled after me, sniffing, and my heart ached in a way I'd never experienced before. I'd been hurt by my mother's lack of interest in my life, ignoring me and my needs my entire life, but my emotions over the past didn't compare to the rawness eating at me from my own heart and Shaylia's close proximity.

A stone sat heavy in my gut as the earth's gravity bore down on my shoulders. I told Damien I would take care of the situation, but I wondered at my ability to do so. The type of hurt both he and Shaylia had experienced from Dee should have bonded them together, not ripped them apart.

I had no question, a wedge worthy of a mighty foe drove between them—my two lovers, the two I didn't want to live without.

Once in my car and headed north, I reached for Shaylia's clasped hands on her lap and weaved my fingers through her trembling ones. At least her tears had stopped.

"Talk to me," I murmured, turning my focus back on the road.

It took a mile of tense silence before she opened her mouth.

"Damien. He's the boy I've compared myself to my entire life. The one I could never live up to, the one who stole my father from us." Her voice caught, and she turned to look out the passenger window.

I'd heard the story before, but her words caused a fresh surge of grief through my empathetic ability.

"Damien never once mentioned Dee had another family."

I felt Shaylia's stare and glanced at her. Brow furrowed and eyes still wet, she peered at me.

"I'm not lying," I said, turning my focus back on the road. "I've been with him since college, Shaylia. There's nothing he hasn't told me."

"You're sure about that?" she asked, her voice soft, disbelieving.

"Yes." I nodded, my mind set on that belief. "What would be his reason for hiding that from me? He must not have known."

She turned back to the window.

"You never knew Damien's name?" I asked as the question rose in my mind.

"No." Shaylia heaved a sigh. "I was only eight when we found out, and I was heartbroken enough my daddy left us. My mom buried our past to protect me, I guess."

"You never asked?"

"I overheard my mother sobbing over the phone to her best friend the day she found out. I knew my father had a stepson—a *rich* one, a smart one. That had been enough to make me realize I hadn't been enough. I couldn't bear the thought of learning more."

I squeezed her fingers, once more at a loss of what to say.

Chapter 32

Shaylia

Ethan pulled into my driveway, and I grabbed my purse, ready for some distance—silence.

I hopped out before he could climb from the car and open my door like he usually did, meeting him in front of the car which he'd turned off.

"Can I come in?" he asked, his voice low and uncertain.

I met his gaze, studied his green eyes, recognizing hurt and disappointment. While I wanted to wallow in the shitty pig sty of my life, I couldn't stand the thought of Ethan hurting. "Okay."

I let us in, tossed my purse on the table, and yanked the bottle of white from the fridge. I poured two glasses without asking him if he wanted any, and we sat on the couch. One long swallow chilled my mouth and throat but did nothing to ease the heaviness in my mind.

"I've never been so devastated in my life," I murmured, realizing the hurt in my heart went beyond that of what I'd felt as a child. "Betrayed all over again by the same damn man."

"You mean Damien." He didn't voice the words as a question.

I nodded, anyway and took another swallow of wine while kicking off my heels.

"It wasn't his fault," Ethan murmured, tucking my hair behind my ear, his hand lingering to cup my cheek.

"It was my father's fault," I said, knowing that truth as I had for years once my adult brain had made sense of my childhood trauma. "But that truth hasn't been able to eradicate the deep-rooted hatred of the person who he replaced me with."

I met Ethan's steady gaze, the warmth in his eyes soothing me the slightest bit as his thumb brushed over my cheekbone. "I'm glad you're here," I said. "I'm glad you can feel what I'm going through."

"More than you know." His wry grin didn't lessen the pain etched on his face.

"I'm sorry, Ethan. I—"

He captured my lips with a gentle kiss, his soft touch sending an ache through my chest. "Don't ever apologize for how you feel, Shaylia," he murmured, tipping his forehead to mine, his palm still holding my cheek. "I love that I can feel you."

Ethan pulled back, his gaze flickering from one of my eyes to the other. "I love you. You're the first person to show an interest in me. My dreams. My desires. You make me feel special."

My breath caught, and I swallowed, hurt on a whole new level. "I love you, too," I admitted, my heart aching at his growing smile, "but that love will ruin what you have with Damien."

Ethan set his wine aside and reached for my hand. "It doesn't have to."

I pulled away and stood, hugging myself with one arm. "I can't do this with him—I can't."

"We can work this out, Shaylia."

I shook my head, my eyes welling with tears again. "He's the one, Ethan. He's the one who made me what I am. *Who* I am. I strove for perfection all my life because I wasn't good enough in my father's eyes."

Ethan opened his mouth, but I plowed onward.

"I've hated Damien for years even though I didn't know his name, even though I'd only ever seen his picture once."

"Please, Shaylia." Ethan stood and reached for me, and I couldn't bear to look into his eyes any longer.

"I can't."

"I'll choose you if I must."

I jerked my head up again. "Don't put me in between the two of you. Please. I-I love you too much to allow you to do such a thing."

He blinked, and I wondered how my love for Ethan overshadowed my hatred for Damien that I wouldn't rip them apart and keep the better half for myself.

"Damien is more than a brother to you." My voice caught, and I swallowed against the thickness in my throat. "You are bonded to one another in ways most partners aren't."

Ethan searched my face from the short distance between us. "You don't hate him."

A sob escaped as more tears rolled down my face. Of course, Ethan knew my growing feelings toward Damien—but they needed to change now that the truth of who he was had come out.

"I can't do this, Ethan. I'm sorry."

He studied me for a few moments before pursing his lips and nodding.

I turned to my door and opened it, a warm breeze full of the scent of sweet summer flowers wafting past my face. Breathing deeply allowed me to grasp control of my messed up emotions enough, I could once more meet Ethan's gaze without losing my shit and breaking down.

"This isn't over," he murmured, once on my stoop, turning to face me.

A tear slid down my cheek, and the smile lifting my lips was only meant to ease the hurt I'd caused him. "I'm sorry."

I turned and shut the door, closing the chapter of my life where I'd felt special—accepted for me, faults and all. The short time I'd had with Ethan and Damien had fulfilled me in unexpected ways.

Even though Ethan had claimed he would choose me, I knew given time, he would realize Damien's hold on his heart trumped that of mine, a mere girlfriend of only a few weeks. I would come in second place in Ethan's heart every time—he just hadn't realized that truth yet.

Chapter 33

Damien

I emptied the flask from my bottom drawer down my throat while staring at the smashed mugs and coffee on the floor. Numbness eventually crept into my brain, easing the anger, the reiterated sense of betrayal.

I'd been so fucking sure Dee had sent Shaylia to fuck with me since I'd helped put him behind bars. Ethan claimed it wasn't possible, not long after I'd held Dee by his goddamn throat, demanding the truth, and he'd said the same.

Scrubbing a hand over my face, I cursed myself for nearly choking an already dying man—even if I did want to end his goddamn life. Knowing it would have been an easier death than cancer's slow suck of whatever days Dee had remaining, I'd released my hold. By the time he'd told me what I'd wanted to know, I lamented not snapping his neck.

Shaking with barely suppressed rage, I released my hold on Dee and tossed him back into his chair.

"Tell me," I demanded through gritted teeth. "Tell me the truth about this fucked-up situation you've created."

He coughed twice, rubbing his neck, not meeting my gaze. "Shaylia was three when I met your mother and married her," he said, his voice hoarse.

"Sick fuck," I muttered, my hands fisting at my sides.

"I-I was married to both women for five years before her mom found out." Dee folded his bony hands on his lap and kept his focus lowered. "It had been Shaylia who brought the truth of my sins to light."

I snorted but didn't say a word.

"She found a picture of you, your mom, and me in my wallet and showed it to her mother. I admitted the

truth of what had been burdening my soul all those years, and I didn't contest the divorce or fight for visitation rights."

"Fucking bastard," I muttered, hating that hurt for Shaylia layered atop mine in my heart.

"I've paid for my sins and then some."

"Not nearly enough," I said through clenched teeth, happy cancer ate away at his body. "Why didn't you ever tell mom and me about your other life?"

"Because I'm a selfish fucking bastard," Dee half-repeated me in a matter-of-fact tone of a man forced to face his fate.

I stared down at him, my body still shaking. "You fucking hid the truth from us and stole from my grandfather's company. Drove our name near to shit."

Dee finally lifted his cowardly face. "I came here to apologize for all I've done, all the heartache I've caused. I've led a double life, lied, and stole from your family—I willingly admit my sins."

"There's no god or priest on this goddamn earth who can absolve you of your sins, and I sure as hell won't."

I strode to the door which still stood open from Shaylia's escape and Ethan's rushing after her. "Get the fuck out."

Dee moved past me without a word, his shoulders stooped.

The hallway laid empty, and I glared at the wisps of white hair atop his head until the elevator dinged shut behind him.

I grabbed my cell and shot a text to Ethan, letting him know I was going back to the condo. I wondered when —if—he would meet me there.

Would Shaylia, like her father, hurt me by manipulating Ethan into staying with her?

My gut twisted into a painful knot as I pocketed my cell, grabbed my keys, and exited my office.

Madeline's head jerked toward me. "Mr. Fiorenza?"

I focused on the elevator and getting the hell away from the office but paused to fill in the faithful woman who had stuck with my family through our near downfall.

"Dee is Shaylia's father," I said, pulling up short alongside her desk.

"*What*?" she gasped, her eyes widening.

"It's a long fucking story," I muttered. "One for another time, but I know she hasn't had contact with him since she was a child."

"That poor girl," Madeline murmured, her brow furrowing.

I hated I thought the same fucking thing, and my jaw clenched. "Ethan took her home. I'm leaving for the day," I managed to say through my teeth.

"What a mess," Madeline said softly, compassion etching her face.

"One that won't clean up as easily as that fucking coffee tray on my floor."

"I'll take care of it, Mr. Fiorenza," she said, her voice low as she stood and patted my forearm, moving toward my office. "Take yourself home. I'm sure things will work out for the best in the end."

For the best...

For me, Ethan, or Shaylia?

I hailed a cab rather than drive half-drunk and wondered the entire way back to the condo whose best interest fate had decided on.

Chapter 34

Ethan

Having received Damien's text, I headed home rather than go back to the office after leaving Shaylia's. For the first time in my life, I wanted to get rip-roaring drunk—numb to the pain in my heart and the lingering effects of both Shaylia's and Damien's hurt.

I cursed my empathy in ways I never had before. I hated that part of my mother I'd inherited with a new heated fervor.

She'd always insisted our purpose, our value came from helping people, and that one heart-to-heart I'd had with her had shaped my life. Made me believe I had no value since I couldn't stand dealing with emotions other than my own—until I'd met Damien and Shaylia, neither who I'd felt needed me emotionally.

Probably why I'm so drawn to them. But now...

I heaved a breath, thinking I finally had a chance to use my abilities for good beyond reading potential clients and employees.

Damien sat on the couch in his slacks and button-down, his tie askew, his hair a spiked mess. He held a bottle of vodka by the neck and lifted it toward me the second I walked into the condo. Drunk and numb, he didn't knife me with the emotional outpour I'd expected.

Without a word, I moved toward him and guzzled, my throat burning, my stomach roiling.

"Where is she?" Damien asked, his voice slurred.

"Home."

He nodded and held out his hand.

I passed the bottle back to him, watching his throat bob as he swallowed. Shifting on my feet, I considered what to say, and couldn't come up with a damn thing.

"I let her in, Ethan," Damien finally muttered, and I let out the breath I hadn't realized I'd been holding.

"I know," I replied, my voice low.

"Gave her fucking power over me without even realizing it." Damien swallowed another mouthful, his upper body swaying, his eyes glazed. "Now, I'm fucking *wrecked*."

"Give me that," I said, reaching for the bottle.

"Don't fucking tell me what to do!" He stood and stumbled, fire brewing in his eyes, his anger and hurt like a sickening sludge oozing through his pores past the numbness he'd cloaked himself in.

"Damien—"

He grabbed hold of my shirt and shoved me backward, stumbling along after me, the bottle in his other hand. "You're mine," he growled in my face, slamming me against the wall. "She's not going to take you away from me."

"I love you both. I *want* you both," I told him the only truth I knew, the truth enforced as my body responded to his show of dominance, his declaration of love in the only way he knew how.

"You can't *have* both," he said, his gaze hard and unwavering even though copious amounts of alcohol rushed through his system. "She hates me, and I won't let her in again."

At that moment, I hated that I loved him, hated he would force a decision on me without voicing the words. His hurt fed the anger lancing out from him, and I found my eyes welling with tears.

"Please don't make me choose," I whispered.

Damien clenched his eyes shut, his brow furrowed. "I can't lose you, Ethan. Can't fucking live without you."

"Say it, Damien. Say what you really mean."

"I fucking love you, Ethan," he groaned, his forehead tipping against mine. "I've loved you since the first time I fucking saw you. You're the best part of me, the only thing—"

I smashed my lips to his, cutting him off, my heart overwhelmed and broken, at the same time.

Damien dropped the bottle, glass shards and vodka splattering our shoes, but neither of us paid it any heed as he grabbed hold of my face and took control, eating at my mouth—devouring and claiming, showing me the truth of his words.

He pressed his body against mine, trapping me to the wall, but at that moment, I didn't wish to escape.

"Need you," I said into his mouth. "Please, Damien."

With a growl, he tore away and yanked me toward the bedroom. Gazes locked, Damien swaying, we stripped and came together again, both of us groaning as our dicks strained against each other.

"On your back," Damien said, stepping away. "I want to see your face when I fuck you."

I scrambled onto the bed, my mouth dry as he grabbed the lube from the bed stand and stroked his hard length, oozing pre-cum from its head.

He settled between my spread thighs, and I pulled my knees to my chest, needing him so bad, my insides quivered. Unable to catch my breath, I panted as he pressed the head of his dick against my hole.

"I love you, Ethan," he said, his passion and vodka-hazed eyes peering into mine. "Fucking love you."

I relaxed as he flexed his ass, one slow glide seating him deep inside my body. We groaned at the same time.

"Love you," I managed before he claimed my mouth, pouring his emotion into me with every thrust of his hips.

We climaxed together, the heat of him releasing inside me jerking my dick between our stomachs, milking my balls dry.

"I'm so sorry," Damien murmured against my neck as we came down. "So fucking sorry for never telling you how much I love you. For never showing you."

I squeezed him tightly to me, uncaring of the cum smeared between us. "I'm never leaving you," I assured him, knowing that truth in my heart—but I wasn't yet willing to let Shaylia go.

There had to be a way to make things right. I just hoped time would heal the wounds Shaylia's father had inflicted on both of them. Knowing Shaylia's hurt and Damien's stubbornness, however, I expected I would have a mental *and* emotional fight on my hands.

* * *

Damien passed out shortly after we showered together, and I watched him sleep, the furrow between his brows smoothed, his breathing soft and relaxed. My heart swelled at the memory of his words, the claiming of my body, but I felt Shaylia's absence in our bed just as keenly.

I rolled and retrieved my cell off my bed stand, texting her the only thing I could at that moment.

Me: **I love you.**

Knowing she wouldn't reply, I put my cell back down and curled once more to face Damien, closing my eyes in the hope sleep would ease my mind as it had his. The oppressive silence laid heavy on me, and while the peacefulness of our bedroom should have helped me figure out the emotional mess in my head and memory, I failed.

* * *

Shaylia didn't come into work—not that either of us expected her to. Damien called me at the gallery, letting me know of the short, professional email she'd sent him, saying she quit. He sounded relieved, but I refused to get angry at him for attempting to protect his heart.

She hadn't included anything personal, simply a two-sentence goodbye, one that broke my heart anew.

I managed to hold off from calling her until ten. Surprised she answered, it took me a few seconds to find my voice.

"Shaylia," I said, my chest squeezing like a vise clamped around me.

"Hi."

"I can't be here at the gallery without you crossing my mind every other minute," I blurted, pacing the small room out back. "I made a sale already this morning, and my heart ached you weren't here to help me celebrate."

"Ethan—"

"Tell me what I can do to make things right, Shaylia. Please. I'll do anything."

"I can't forgive him," she whispered, her voice breaking.

I stopped pacing, closed my eyes, and tilted my head back. "It wasn't Damien. It was Dee."

"I know that, I do, but I-I can't let that go."

"Time, Shaylia. In time, you can."

"I'm proud of you," she said, a smile sounding through her wavering voice. "But this is goodbye, Ethan."

She hung up, and I collapsed at the table and swallowed against sobs—a battle I quickly lost.

Chapter 35

Shaylia

As the hours and eventually, days passed, my emotions ranged from bitterness to anger to heartache, jumping from one to the other like a tennis ball between two Olympians.

I drank too much wine and wallowed too many minutes away in self-pity when I should have been searching for another job since I'd quit the temp agency before they could fire me for leaving Fiorenza Financial without a two-week notice.

Fiorenza—the family name of the boy my father had abandoned me for. I'd found out much too late to protect myself.

Tears long-dried, I sat on my couch, staring at the TV and a stupid soap opera I didn't follow, tuning it out.

I couldn't but help question everything that had taken place over the previous few weeks. Had Damien known who I was from day one? Had he agreed to Ethan's suggestion of a threesome merely in hopes of making me fall in love with him in order to hurt the daughter of the man who had hurt him so many years ago?

Wondering about Damien's play in the whole affair ate at me, affirming my belief men in authority lied through their damn teeth. Knowing I needed to move on, I didn't call Ethan to question the truth of the thoughts whirling through my brain. I expected he would deny it, and who would blame him? He'd been with Damien for fifteen years, and the history between them wouldn't be easily forgotten.

Chances were, Damien manipulated him as well to keep him close—tied together where Damien could profit from his lover.

Anger swelled, and I grumbled a few curses.

If I loved Ethan, why not fight for him? Why not fight the bastard who had hurt me? Why not wreck *his* world?

Because you were falling for him too.

"Damnit." Lips pursed, I got up, hating that damn angel on my shoulder, spewing the truth of my emotions. I didn't want to love the man who had shaped me from childhood. I didn't want to even like him or the pleasant memories of him relaying in my mind.

Duck tour.

Dinners.

Sharing Ethan with him, feeling bonded—connected—to both in a way I'd never thought possible with a single man, let alone two.

My cell rang, and my heart jumped to my throat, thinking it might be Ethan again, and I would hit the ignore button—again.

Mom.

"Hey," I said, actually smiling when answering.

"Sweetheart. I haven't talked to you in weeks!" She let out a huff as though she'd been scrubbing or vacuuming, both loves I'd inherited from her.

"Sorry..."

"How is that young man you told me about? Things still going well? I've been dying over here, waiting for an update!"

I laughed lightly over my mother's enthusiasm over my falling in love even though my chest ached. "We broke up."

Silence rang in my ears for a few seconds.

"What?"

I spilled the truth about Ethan having an ex, a man I ended up getting involved with as well—before everything dumped into hell.

"Damien's last name is Fiorenza," I finally added, topping that cake with a pile of shit since she would recognize the name I hadn't known as a child.

"No!" Mom breathed the word, her distress obvious over the phone.

"Of all the people, right?" Sarcastic laugher caught in my throat as it thickened.

"Oh, sweetheart, I'm so sorry."

"So am I, Mom," I whispered, clenching my eyes shut against the tears. "But that's not all. I saw Dad."

Again, silence settled between us.

"He's out of jail and came to the office—I'm assuming to apologize to Damien or something."

"He's dying," Mom murmured.

I should have been upset, a good daughter would have been.

"He looked ... old."

"Pancreatic cancer," Mom said, her voice low but emotionless.

I couldn't find it in my heart to care either.

"Did you ever forgive him, Mom? I mean,"—I opened my eyes and glared at the two actors making out on the TV—"did you ever even consider it?"

"I've accepted what happened, but I don't think I'll ever be able to forgive him for what he did to us."

"And Damien?"

"What about him?"

"Have you forgiven him and his mother for stealing Dad away from us?"

"Dee never told them, Shaylia." Mom sighed. "And I never took it upon myself to be a bitch and confront his other wife."

I picked at lint on my leggings. "Maybe, you should have."

"And maybe I never should have married your father, to begin with, but if I hadn't, I wouldn't have had you."

My throat thickened again.

"We make decisions, good and bad," Mom said, "and while the results sometimes hurt, we need to make the best of them. Learn and grow."

"I need to start over," I murmured the thought as it came to my head. "Find something, or someone, to help close up the hole the loss of both men left inside me."

"Perhaps you ought to focus on yourself for a while first."

Create a better version of myself by going back to school even if it means a pile of debt.

"I'm thinking about taking night classes online," I said, the second the thought finished in my head.

"Oh, sweetheart, I think that's a wonderful idea! I can help you a little with tuition costs."

We chatted for a few more minutes, and by the time we hung up, I decided I would become the best me I could, one who *would* be enough for a change. I would find my own interests, search out things that made *me* happy.

Beneath my hope and my drive to become more, though, I feared failure. I feared I would never find someone as sweet as Ethan, someone as endearing as Damien—even if he was a manipulative liar like my father had been.

"Damnit, Shaylia," I muttered to myself while booting up my laptop to look into online college courses. "Focus on yourself. You don't need a man."

While I spoke the truth, my heart didn't agree.

Chapter 36

Damien

The new temp sent to work with Madeline sucked, but even if she'd been a mirror image of Shaylia, she wouldn't have *been* Shaylia—and I still wouldn't have liked her.

Ethan spent more time in the gallery than the office, so he didn't seem to mind the new girl too much. I knew he missed Shaylia as much as I did though, especially in our bed. We'd fucked a handful of times, but the sexual energy between us lacked since that hate-fuck the night the shit hit the fan, the night I finally found the balls to tell him I loved him.

I told him every morning, every night since, I loved him —and not to keep him from running to Shaylia either.

Having finally vocalized my need for him in my life, my emotions toward him, I felt connected to him on an even deeper level.

Our dicks still took an interest in one another, but something sorely lacked.

I blamed Shaylia for that, too, hardening my heart toward her even more. That, combined with the fact I knew Ethan continued to text her, and she ignored him, put extra bricks on the wall in my mind, keeping away all emotion other than anger toward her.

She was nothing more than a cold-hearted bitch, more concerned with her own heart than that of the man we both supposedly loved.

Kettle ... black.

Cursing the words in my head, I grabbed a folder, only to have Madeline buzz me.

"Mr. Jackson would like to see you if you have a moment."

"Send him in."

Jackson had only been with us as an advisor for a few months, but I liked his work ethic—and Ethan had given a firm stamp of approval on his personality and motive for joining the Fiorenza team.

His brow furrowed as he walked in, a roll of papers in his hand. While I didn't have empathic abilities like Ethan, I knew something bothered the man.

"What's up?" I asked, motioning toward the chair across from me.

He sat and handed the papers over without a word.

"What's this?" I asked, thumbing through them, but I quickly caught on before Jackson said a word. "What the fuck?" I jerked my head up to study him. "How did you get these?"

He held my stare while I'd expected him to shift his gaze away out of guilt for snooping. "Twice, I caught Mr. Setters scrambling to cover up files when I entered his cubicle. While I'm not normally a suspicious person, I had a feeling he was up to no good. I took it upon myself to get to the bottom of it before bothering you with a mere hunch."

"Fuck," I muttered again, glancing down again at the photocopied papers showing Setters had been selling investments that didn't exist. Fraud—similar to what

Dee had done, what had almost ruined us once before. "Does Setters know you have these?"

"No."

The papers revealed Setters had made a shit ton of money—all from our oldest client, one who had remained faithful after Fiorenza Financial's name had smeared across the media. A shit ton of money...

Brow furrowed, I studied the papers for another minute.

"Thank you for this, Jackson," I said, shoving the evidence into my top drawer. "I'll take care of things from here. I appreciate your honesty, and I promise to keep how these papers came to my attention to myself."

Jackson nodded and left.

I buzzed Madeline, telling her to call Setters to my office immediately.

The firm's top financial advisor waltzed in with confidence like he usually did, his suave smile pissing me the hell off.

"Have a seat," I ordered, my tone firm. He did as told, holding my stare—his grin slowly fading. "I know about Mr. Gerson's account."

Setters' face paled, and before he could sputter whatever he tried to voice, I continued.

"You will resign, effective immediately, and I want you out of this building within the hour."

"Mr. Fiorenza." He tried for a grin and cleared his throat, sitting on the edge of the chair. "I'm not sure I understand."

The muscle in my jaw ticking, I sat back in my chair, my gaze hard. "Selling investments that don't exist is a crime, Setters."

"I don't know what you're talking about."

I pulled the papers back out of my top drawer and tossed them across my desk.

He glanced down at the one closest to him and swallowed again, his face taking on a sickened pallor.

"My stepfather's fraudulent activities nearly ruined me," I said, struggling to keep my tone level. "And you would think to do the same after all these years of hard work putting us back on top?"

"No one has to know, Mr. Fiorenza," Setters hurried to say, finally shifting on the chair. "We can keep this quiet—I can give you half of what I've taken."

Mr. Gerson was a billionaire, one without a direct heir to his fortune. Stealing money from the old man had been easy for his financial advisor—too easy.

"Seventy-five percent," Setters pushed.

I hadn't realized I'd paused—that for a split second, I had considered his offer to cover his actions up.

A shit ton of money...

My stomach churned as I considered the amount of cash I'd invested in the London firm, the starting costs of getting the new location up and running. Even a quarter of what Setters had stolen would put the office above water.

"Mr. Fiorenza..."

Mind twisting over right and wrong, I studied him. Dee had taken advantage of his position of authority, and the memory of the outcome knifed my gut. I would not be like him. I would not take an easy route to riches. I would not steal or take advantage of those who entrusted me with their business.

And I also wouldn't hide from the truth or brush under the rug what had happened—no matter the cost.

Holding Setter's gaze, I buzzed Madeline. "Get Mr. Gerson on the phone, please," I said and clicked off the intercom.

"Mr. Fiorenza—"

My glare cut Setters off. "You're going to confess to Mr. Gerson what you've been doing," I said. "You're going to give his money back even if you have to sell every last *fucking* thing you own in order to do so. Are we clear?"

He licked his lip. "You're not going to call the authorities?" he asked, his voice ragged.

"That's for Mr. Gerson to decide."

Setters muttered a few curses, and I steadied myself for the shit storm sure to follow. I questioned the wisdom of my choice over the fallout, but peace over having done the right thing eased me enough, I knew we would somehow make it through again.

Chapter 37

Ethan

Two months without seeing Shaylia—eight long as hell weeks of not hearing her voice or feeling her emotions —drained the joy in life out of me.

Damien sulked. I brooded.

We rarely fucked.

Feeling heavier in my mind than I had for years, I locked up the gallery and headed home, heartbroken when I should have been excited about the art show Damien and I planned to attend that evening.

Trevor and Jack, the two artists I'd admired for almost five years, would be in attendance, something they rarely did, even at their own shows. The two partners led a quiet life, staying out of the limelight. If I'd had the success they did, I would do the same.

I arrived home first and hopped in the shower after a quick bite to eat.

The absence of Shaylia in the condo, even though she'd only been with us a handful of nights, still hit hard, the depression eating at my brain, tempting me to stay in for the night.

Crowds bothered me badly enough without the added unhappiness weighing on my mind. Adding a slew of others' emotions on top of mine didn't appeal—at all.

The bathroom door opened before I finished, and Damien climbed into the shower with me, his tumbling emotions rolling over me. I set the bar of soap aside as his dark-eyed gaze pierced mine.

"What?" I whispered, and he stepped in close, wrapping his arms around me, his forehead on my shoulder. Not sure what to say, I held him tight, wishing like hell he would talk so I could help him with what bothered him.

"Setters has been stealing from Mr. Gerson," Damien finally said, and my breath caught.

"What?"

"Selling him investments that don't exist."

My stomach plummeted as the severity of the situation slammed into my brain. "Oh, *shit*."

Damien explained all that had happened—and what he'd chosen to do about it.

"I'm so proud of you," I said, squeezing him tighter, rather than ask how Mr. Gerson had responded. "You made the right choice."

He exhaled a heavy sigh.

"So, how fucked are we?" I asked while grimacing.

"Not at all."

I stepped back so I could see Damien's face.

His lopsided smile warmed me more than the hot spray against my back. "Initially, Mr. Gerson was pissed and tore Setters a new asshole, but once he calmed down..." Damien's smile faded, and he swallowed, the rush of bitter happiness from him stinging my eyes along with his. "He said my family has been through enough, and he won't press charges because he respects my family. Respects the decision I made to be honest and upfront."

I let out a whoosh of breath. "Oh, thank fuck."

"Tell me about it." Damien heaved a sigh and stretched his neck side to side. "I need a goddamn drink."

"Want to stay home tonight and get drunk off our asses to celebrate?" I asked, hoping he would agree.

"Nope." Damien spun us, his back toward the water. "It took a couple of phone calls to find my cousin, and I had to promise her my first born, but I got those damn tickets, and we're going. We'll celebrate with champagne rather than vodka. And when we get home..."

A glint lit his eye, one I'd been missing, one that twitched my dick.

He palmed my flaccid length, quickly bringing blood to swell it fully. "When we get home," he murmured, lowering his lips a breath from mine, "I'm going to get on my knees and worship you."

"Fuck." I groaned, my head tipping back as he squeezed.

"Oh, I'll do that too." He released his hold and swatted my thigh. "Go put on that tux. The one I'm going to rip off you later tonight."

We met Trevor and Jack—and the gorgeous blonde between them, hanging on both their arms, who happened to be best friends with one of Damien's cousins. The connection I'd never known about, the cousin I certainly wanted to hug.

My insides warmed, not just from meeting the two men, but from the happiness on their faces and the inner joy radiating off all three of them—a relationship of three, a strong one for over five years, from what the tabloids spouted.

Three is possible.

My throat clogged, and I sipped my champagne to ease its ache at seeing their easiness with each other.

"We painted *Perfection* for Meg," Jack said, his eyes shining with love at the woman who oozed affection in return.

Damien shifted at my side, and I forced myself to focus on those around me rather than the what-might-bes or what-ifs.

"I've admired your work for some time," I said, my gaze flitting between the two men, jealousy eating at me, alongside my heartache. "You're very lucky."

Trevor laughed lightly, and his wife smiled up at him.

"More like they were so damn persistent," she said, "I gave in just to shut them up."

Jack chuckled, and while I smiled, I didn't feel a single ounce of joy. "Damien here, told us that you have a gallery downtown?"

My heart stalled and kicked into high gear a second later. "Yes," I managed to answer, my voice rasped.

"We would love to stop in some time," Jack said without a trace of negative emotions to make me think he had just tossed his words out as small talk.

Excitement and happiness spiked—both mine and Damien's. Through shaky laughter, I told them where to find my hole-in-the-wall gallery. Damien pulled one of my cards from his back pocket and handed it to Jack, and the thoughtfulness of his gesture—the fact he'd brought my cards with him when I hadn't even thought to do so—warmed my heart.

My throat thickened, and when the threesome left us to mingle with other guests, overwhelming love for my partner had me tugging his hand toward the exit.

Chapter 38

Shaylia

I floated through life, my emotions numbed by keeping busy. A doctor's office kept my mind occupied during the day, phones and patients giving me something other than myself to focus on. Evening online courses kept the loneliness away, and I studied until passing out in my bed, every single night.

It was a random online news ad that caught my eye—and not the headline about the art world's greatest duo. It was the two men alongside them, holding champagne and talking to the two—and the woman between them—who held my stare.

My heart ached, broke anew, but I couldn't tear my focus off Damien and Ethan. They stood close, shoulders brushing, and I wondered about their happiness. I expected Ethan rode cloud nine that evening a week prior. He'd been looking forward to the art show for months.

I wondered as well at the third ticket Damien had managed to obtain, one that had been meant for me.

Swallowing back disappointment, I wondered over my lack of anger at seeing Damien's face.

On a whim, I opened another tab and started digging through cyber space.

Pictures of him as a young man along with his mother and my father squeezed my chest, but I forced myself to focus on his face.

Happiness—admiration for the man he peered at— showed on his youthful face. Two other pictures revealed the same. Damien Fiorenza had loved my father, had accepted him into his life, exactly as he'd told me.

The wretched pain etched in his eyes as a young man in court sent a twinge of discomfort through me. Damien appeared devastated.

His mother divorced my father before the court proceedings even finished, placing my father in jail.

Fiorenza Financial had been dragged to the edge of ruination. While Damien hadn't shared details of how his stepfather had nearly ruined his grandfather's company and name, I'd heard the pain in his voice.

We shared the same hurt—betrayal by the man we most looked up to. A father figure meant to watch over us, protect us from those who abused the power of authority.

A slew of emotions swirled through me, and the need for answers drove me to call Mom.

"Hi, sweetheart."

I broke down sobbing, and it was some time before I finally asked for my father's number. Encouraged by my mother, I hung up and immediately called him, my heart thumping harshly in my chest.

"It's Shaylia," I managed when he answered.

"Shaylia." His voice caught, and I swallowed. I hadn't spoken to him since I was eight, and the sudden burden of the pain I'd carried in my heart exploded.

"Why did you do it?" I blurted, tears welling. "Was I not enough?"

"Oh, Shay." My father broke down, the pain in his voice hitting me hard. "You were an angel, baby. A perfect little girl."

"Then, why?" I asked, my voice raising as I fisted my free hand and strode across my narrow living room. "Why?"

"Selfishness." He sniffed. "Greed. I-I saw a chance to make big money, and I took advantage of a new widow and her young son."

Anger and my lifelong bitterness festered even though the ache of my lacking self-identity eased the slightest bit. I glanced down at my laptop, at the picture of Damien gazing up at him with adoration.

"Did you love Damien as your own?"

"Not nearly as much as I did you," he said, his quiet tone full of grief.

"You hurt him the same as you hurt me."

"I've hurt so many people, and the guilt of having done so eats at me with a pain deeper than any cancer."

My throat thickened. My father faced imminent death by a disease that couldn't be cured. Pity laced through my pain and the hurt that still festered in my heart.

"I'm choosing to forgive you," I whispered, my throat thick, "but I don't want you in my life."

He exhaled heavily. "Thank you, baby girl."

I hung up before a sob let loose and gave over to the vortex of emotions swirling through me. Rather than guzzle wine or seek numbness through distraction, I allowed my feelings to have their way with me until my tears drained dry.

Chapter 39

Damien

Mr. Gerson stopped by the office unexpectedly on Monday morning, his personal assistant bringing along coffees for the two of us—the good stuff, he claimed with a chuckle.

Once settled in the chair across from me, Mr. Gerson set his watery-eyed gaze on me, and I fought not to shift beneath his stare. While he'd told me on Friday he had no wish to see my firm taken through the ringer again, I wondered at his visit, my stomach in knots.

"You're a good man, Damien."

I held my breath, waiting for his "but."

"You're a young whipper-snapper, but your grandfather taught you well, God rest his soul." He clutched his cane in one hand, the other holding tight to his coffee cup. "I'm proud to say I do business with Fiorenza Financial."

My breath left in a rush. "Thank you, Mr. Gerson. You have no idea how much I apprec—"

"But that Setters fellow." His sparse eyebrows pulled together, and my anxiety spiked again. "I can't have him taking advantage of others the way he did to me."

"I understand, Mr. Gerson," I said, pleased I kept my tone level rather than it shake with the adrenaline rushing through me at what I knew was coming.

"I've spoken with my lawyers."

I waited, breath once more held.

"And we've decided to give the bastard time to make good on his promise to repay—with interest—what he stole from me."

I nodded, my heart still in my throat.

"There will be no mention to the media, no whisperings of fraud. Mr. Setters is meeting with us this afternoon to sign an agreement, one that will ensure he sticks to his word and keeps this whole business under wraps."

Relief rushed through me, and unable to voice a word, I nodded.

"You're a good man, a bright one." Mr. Gerson grunted while standing, his short height putting him eye level with me while I sat. "You're going to be an even greater one—you've got many years left to accomplish your goals."

"I-I can only hope fate will be kind, sir," I said, rising to my feet.

"No hoping about it, son," Mr. Gerson huffed a snort and tapped his cane on the floor. "Just doing."

A smile twitched my lips at his surety and stubborn tone. "Are you saying I should *make* it happen?" I asked.

He nodded, the wrinkled skin around his eyes crinkling even deeper.

"Go out and grab whatever you want by the balls, young man. Take it and own it." He pointed his cane at me and winked. "I did that with business but ignored my personal life when I should have been loving on a woman and creating a family. I'm an old codger now. A lonely one," he said with a chuckle, turning toward the door. "Don't make the same mistakes I did."

"Yes, sir."

Mr. Gerson pulled up by my door and tottered to face me once more. "It takes more than fame and fortune to fulfill a man. Take it from one who knows."

He left me standing in my office—alone—my mind full.

For a moment, I had considered doing as Dee had done—actually considered lying by omission and stealing from a generous old man who I thought had it all.

Mr. Gerson trusted me, a much-younger man in authority.

I'd made the right decision, protecting his assets at the possible expense of my name.

Self-pride swelled through me, but not in the way that made me want to shout from the rooftops of the great thing I'd done. I didn't want praise, I didn't want admiration.

I wanted a hell of a lot more.

* * *

After work, I headed north, my GPS leading me to a small bungalow rental, drab brown and sad-looking beneath the saturated trees bowing over it. Shoulders hunched against the drizzle falling since mid-morning, I hurried to the front stoop and knocked, my heart racing.

The second the door opened, I shoved the dozen pink roses in my hand in front of Shaylia's face.

She gaped up at me, holding tight to the door knob, her other hand at her side. "What are you doing here?"

"To beg you for a second chance."

Shaylia glanced at the roses, her face void of emotion, and I wished like fuck for Ethan's ability to tell me what she felt.

"Please, Shay." I swallowed and pushed the roses closer. "We need to sit down and talk. We need to figure this out. Ethan is a mess. I'm a mess." I implored her with my gaze, grasping at goddamn straws.

Lips thinned, she accepted the flowers, but her eyes held no promise when she returned her focus to my face. "I don't know if I can, Damien."

"I know how hard it is to trust." I half-laughed at the absurdity, the ridiculous chances of falling for the one woman who had every right to hate my guts. "I've been hurt too, Shay."

"I know," she whispered, her shoulders relaxing, her gaze dropping once more to the flowers, her subtle scent of vanilla and cherries watering my mouth.

"Would you come to dinner tonight? Sit and hash this shit out—with Ethan too?"

"This isn't his problem."

"It's not, but he holds the key to making things right."

Her head tilted to the side, she studied my face. "How so?"

"We can speak of our honesty out of our asses, but he can assure us of the truth behind our words."

"That's not trusting, Damien."

I nodded, knowing she was right, but I wasn't going to let that stop me. "It's a good start," I said, fighting to keep from pulling her into my arms. "Please, Shay. If you can't do this for yourself or me, at least do it for Ethan. I would give him the world if I could."

"You lowered yourself to begging," Shaylia said with a small smile. "*That's* a good start."

I chuckled, my heart feeling lighter than it had in months even though the skies overhead opened up with a massive bang. "And I'll continue begging until you agree."

"Stubborn mule."

"I am."

"Fine." Shaylia huffed a heavy sigh. "Dinner and conversation—*only*."

I grinned, the heavy rain soaking me through. Thunder rumbled again, and droplets of water fell off the end of my nose. "Seven?"

She nodded, and the upturn of her lips kept me grinning as I scampered back to my car and soaked my leather interior.

Chapter 40

Shaylia

I didn't bother showering or shaving since I had zero intention of allowing either man anywhere beneath my clothing. Remembering my prickly legs would keep me from giving into the sexual draw of both men, regardless of what transpired over dinner.

While I'd sworn to hate the boy who'd stolen my father from me, I had trouble putting Damien's gorgeousness, his hopeful eyes to the face I'd imagined all my life. Soaked like a drowned rat, the man still exuded sexual energy I couldn't brush off.

The desire in his eyes, the fact he'd begged for a chance to make things right had eased my negative thoughts toward him even more.

My entire body trembled climbing the stairs to their condo. I needed the extra time to set my thoughts straight, line up the questions I needed to ask, the things we needed to discuss. With Damien's declaration about Ethan being a key to making things right, I worried over the band aid his abilities might be.

Knowing how Damien truly felt, knowing his true intent, wouldn't fully heal my hurt or cause me to trust him. Ethan's ability to know if someone spoke the truth wouldn't bring to life the type of trust needed for relationships to work. That took faith—a step into the unknown, allowing someone to have the power to possibly re-destroy your heart.

No matter how attractive I found Damien, no matter the sexual compatibility or connection I'd felt with him, I just didn't know if I had that ability to trust again.

Damien answered the door the second I knocked, and my smile wobbled. "Hey."

He stepped back, grinning like a fool. "Thanks so much for this, Shay," he said, motioning me in.

The woodsy scent of his cologne swirled around me, and I swallowed sudden drool.

"Is someone at the door?" Ethan called from the bedroom.

I jerked my focus up to Damien's face. "He doesn't know you invited me over?"

Damien shook his head, his smile faltering briefly. "I didn't tell him—just in case you didn't show."

"Oh." I clutched my purse in front of me, movement from their bedroom door drawing my attention.

"Shaylia," Ethan breathed my name, halting in their doorway. He wore lounge pants low on his hips, droplets of water from the shower clinging to his mussed hair.

"Hey," I croaked, hating yet loving how my body warmed completely through at the sight of his bare skin and sculpted muscles.

He found his feet and hurried toward me, his lush lips curling up in a panty-melting smile. "It's so good to see you," he whispered, drawing close but not touching.

I clutched my purse like a damn shield as the room's crackling energy lifted the hairs on my arms. "You, too."

Ethan glanced at Damien. "This your doing?"

"Yes."

"I don't know who I want to hug more," Ethan said with a shaky laugh.

I tipped my head toward Damien and bit the inside of my lip as Ethan grabbed him and planted a lingering kiss on his lips.

My thighs pressed together on their own, and I readjusted my hold on my shield, squeezing it tighter.

"Wine?" Damien asked, turning into the kitchen.

"Okay," I croaked.

Ethan took my elbow and steered me into the living room. "Did you eat dinner? Damien ordered Thai."

"I haven't, no."

We settled on the couch, mere inches between our knees as we angled to face each other. The scent of his body wash, the close proximity of his skin tingled my fingertips, and I fought the shakes from nervousness—and need.

Ethan studied my face, and I didn't fight the feelings inside me. I didn't bother trying to hide my desire for him or my reservations, my fear, and the hurt that still lingered deep in my heart. "Thank you for coming, Shaylia."

I nodded, and Damien joined us, handing us both a glass of wine. He held out his hand for my shield, and I reluctantly handed my purse over to him.

Ethan let out a heavy sigh as Damien moved back to the kitchen area. "I'll be honest," Ethan said, keeping his voice low, "your combined emotions are tough to wade through."

"I'm sorry."

"Don't be." He smiled although I noted the etching of his brow. "It's my curse, one I've learned to handle."

"But have you learned to appreciate it?" I asked as Damien returned, and I wondered over what he felt.

"He will after tonight," Damien answered before Ethan could, sitting on a chair across from us. He held a glass half-full of ice and clear liquid. A too-tight—yet not tight enough—t-shirt encased the muscles rippling down his front as he sat back, a confident smile on his face. "You're the key to making this mess right again," he said.

Ethan quirked a brow, and I took a decent swallow of wine. The two men oozed sex appeal, lighting up all the right places inside me. Trying to force away memories of being between them and keeping focus on why I'd agreed to dinner didn't come easy.

I looked at Damien, waiting for him since our sit down had been his idea.

He held my stare and sipped before placing his glass on the coffee table between us. Leaning forward, he propped his elbows on his knees. "I thought Dee had sent you to weasel your way into my life and take me down for helping to put him behind bars."

My eyes popped open. "What?"

"But I realized you didn't."

"I would never!"

"I know." He glanced at Ethan before turning back to me. "Because of what Dee did to me, to my family, I have a hard time with authority. I hate anyone to have power over me in any way, shape, or form. Trusting doesn't come easy for me."

I nodded, clutching the glass's stem.

"I agreed to a threesome for Ethan's sake, determined to keep you at arm's length, but you somehow snuck past my walls, Shaylia." His crooked smile rushed butterflies through me. "I hated you for that. Hated that you'd tricked me into giving you power over my emotions."

"I didn't trick you," I whispered, ensnared by his steady gaze.

"I know that now, but it took a lot for me to get that truth through my head. I'm stubborn, as you well know."

We stared at one another, and I couldn't think of how to respond—of what he might want to hear from me.

"I'm not asking you to trust me, Shay," he finally continued, "but I sure as hell would like a chance to *earn* your trust."

Swallowing, I glanced at Ethan, who also stared at Damien. Wetness coated his eyes, and I felt his love for Damien as clearly as my own for him. Pride showed on his profile, and I found myself happy Damien's openness pleased Ethan so much.

Ethan's gaze flicked toward me, and my breath caught at the love in his eyes—not just for Damien, who had flaws galore, but for me as well, a very imperfect woman, one far from being all she wanted to be.

"Everything he said is the truth, Shaylia."

Tears clogged my throat, and I turned back to Damien, ready to spill all the shit in my life, throw it all out. Let him believe what he would, whatever Ethan assured him of. I wasn't an empath, I wasn't perfect—but I believe Ethan accepted me, loved me just the way I was.

"I didn't know your name," I said, my voice shaking, "but I've hated you with a passion since I was eight years old."

Damien's smile faded, and he nodded. "Understandably."

"I always measured myself up to the boy who stole my father from me—who my father *chose* over me, but I learned that wasn't so." Unable to stand the pain in Damien's eyes, I focused on my wine. "I called my father the other day."

Ethan's breath caught, but I kept going.

"I've chosen to forgive him because I needed to in order to move on with my life, but what he did isn't something I'll ever forget. I learned it wasn't you and your mother who took him from me but the selfishness and greed of a sickened soul who I now pity."

"Knowing the truth of what has shaped your life isn't going to make trusting any easier," Ethan spoke what I already knew—what Damien did as well—but having the words between us opened the door. "Both of you are speaking from your hearts," Ethan continued, his voice soft. "Both of you mean every word."

I peered at Damien, who nodded at Ethan as though accepting his affirmation of the truth of my words. He returned his focus to me, and a silent understanding seemed to solidify between us.

"I fear the same vulnerability as you," I whispered to him, "and giving this another shot scares the shit out of me, but I promise I have no intention of hurting you."

"The last thing I want to do is give you a reason not to trust me," Damien replied. "You might be Dee's daughter, but you're nothing like him, Shay. You're a sweetheart, a giving, thoughtful woman I'd like a chance to prove myself to."

Neither of us looked at Ethan for confirmation, and I wondered if the faith to trust a person's word could come so easily.

My shoulders eased, and I let out a big breath as a sense of peace—and rightness—seeped into my soul.

Chapter 41

Ethan

The two people I loved most stared at one another, their hurt fading behind budding hopefulness. Tears hazed my vision, and I fought to keep breathing evenly, waiting for them to look at me for confirmation.

Neither did, and I swallowed against a painful rush of joy in the hope they might trust each other. Damien hadn't been correct—I wasn't the key to making things right between them. Once again, I failed to find value in what my empathic abilities supposedly gave me.

That truth should have hurt more than it did, but with their hopefulness rising on both sides, I shoved my disappointment away.

"I didn't expect to like you, let alone fall for you, but I did," Damien finally broke the stillness among us. "And these past weeks without you—"

"They sucked," I blurted. "We aren't right without out you with us. Between us."

Shaylia turned toward me, her smile hurting my heart.

"You're like the puzzle piece we didn't know was missing from our lives," I added. Damien and I hadn't spoken of such things, but he couldn't hide his feelings from me. He'd missed her just as much as I had.

"You're perfect for us," Damien murmured.

A tear slid down Shaylia's cheek as she turned her attention on him. "I've never felt good enough for anybody before, myself included."

Damien stood and rounded the coffee table to kneel between us. Our fingers twined on instinct, and he held his other hand toward her.

Shaylia's gaze flickered to his hand, to his face, and I held my breath, waiting for her decision to trust. Nothing I could say would make her do so.

"I wouldn't change a damn thing about you," Damien said.

"Me neither," I added.

She set her wine aside and accepted our outstretched hands, creating a circle.

I heaved a heavy sigh, still fighting off tears. "I'm the luckiest bastard alive," I muttered as their emotions swarmed over mine, aligning in ways I hadn't dared to hope.

"I'm the lucky one," Damien said. "It took almost losing you to make me realize what I had. I'm sorry for becoming so familiar, so passive toward our relationship—to *you*—when I should have been loving on you every day."

A huffed snort escaped me. "You *were* loving on me every day."

"You know what I mean," he said with a laugh. "I'd been so caught up in righting the mess Dee had made, I forgot to remind you how much you mean to me, how much my life would suck without you."

"You were there for me when others weren't," I told him. "You were the rock who stood by me, protected me when I got overwhelmed that first year in college. Without you, I wouldn't have made it through school." God, did I want to kiss him, show him how much I appreciated him.

"*I'm* the lucky one," Shaylia said with a sigh. "What woman wouldn't be thrilled to have, not just one hot guy but two, saying I'm perfect the way I am?"

Her happiness poured over me, and I released Damien's hand to pull her into my arms. She smelled of cherries and female, so soft and *right* in my arms.

"God, you smell good," I whispered against her hair, loving how her heart thrummed against my chest.

"You, too," she said with a sigh. "Thank you."

"For?"

"Being the one to bring us together."

"I had nothing to do with it," I huffed. "You two didn't need my empathic abilities to heal the rift between you."

Shaylia pulled back and cupped my cheek. "You're what brought us together, and if not for your special gift, neither Damien nor I would have been willing to talk things through."

I stared, considering her words.

"You've seen your ability as a hindrance your entire life," Damien said, squeezing my hand and drawing my focus, "but it has saved mine. My family."

Tears hazed my vision.

"Your purpose isn't in just helping others though, Ethan," Shaylia said, laying her head against my chest with a sigh. "Your purpose is to be you, to be loved by Damien—by me."

A shuddering sigh rippled through me as Damien's smile wobbled, his gaze full of that love she claimed.

"Let us love you, Ethan. Let me love you, Shaylia," he whispered. "Please."

I grabbed hold of his neck and pulled him close, planting my lips on his.

"God," Shaylia moaned. "You two are so—"

The damn doorbell rang.

"Dinner," Damien said with a groan.

"Forget food," I mumbled, staring at his lips.

"It's already paid for."

"I'll get it," Shaylia said, jumping up and leaving us alone.

Damien held my gaze, his dark eyes full of passion and thankfulness, matching the emotions rolling over me. "I love you, Ethan Lord."

"And I love you, Damien Fiorenza."

He kissed me lightly, a mere tease compared to what I wanted. "After dinner," he said, standing, "we're going to show Shaylia how much we love her."

I wasn't about to argue.

Chapter 42

Damien

I sat in the pre-dawn hours, sipping coffee when I usually would be out running and sweating my ass off.

My two lovers still laid in bed, tangled together, their heavy breaths comforting me. Talking Shaylia into letting us love her had proven difficult, her face turning red when she finally let me tug her jeans off—she hadn't shaved for two weeks, but I didn't give a fuck.

Having lived with a man for fifteen years, hairy legs didn't bother me one bit—Ethan either. Giggling, she gave into our caresses, our begging. I nuzzled her neck, her breasts while Ethan made love to her, but I didn't give her more than two minutes rest to come down from her climax before sliding into her pussy, still soaked from their combined cum.

The connection I'd felt for her had grown while we'd made love—for that's exactly what we'd done. Eyes locked, we moved together, caught up in the emotions Ethan murmured about while stroking himself. We came as one, Shaylia milking me dry while Ethan coated her chest with his cum.

I shifted on the chair and sipped my coffee again.

I hadn't realized I needed more than Ethan to complete my life, but seeing them both in my bed felt so right. Three would be tough, but I knew it could be done. Those two art guys, Trevor and Jack, had made a threesome work for five years, so why not us?

Hell, since Ethan knew our emotions as they flared, he would make wading through misunderstandings ten times easier. He'd always compared himself to his mom and her ability to help people, but his value to both Shaylia and I didn't come from his gift. It came from being Ethan, the submissive man who completed me, the one who adored Shaylia whole-heartedly, who loved without any doubt in his heart.

He stirred, and Shaylia did a few seconds later. Their murmuring reached my ears, but I couldn't make out what they said.

I sipped again, my morning wood taking interest as Ethan rolled, settling her atop him, her round ass draped by the sheet, drawing my focus.

"I can feel you all the way over here, Damien," Ethan said, his voice raised. "Get your ass in this bed. Shaylia wants you too."

"Can't say no to that," I groaned.

Shaylia sighed with a shudder, a sound I'd become well-familiar with, and my dick jerked at the thought of him fucking into her tight pussy.

I palmed my dick and grabbed the lube from the bed stand where I'd left it the night before. Once slickened, I climbed onto the bed behind them and yanked the sheet off the bed.

Ethan thrust, jiggling Shaylia's ass, and I groaned, working myself while watching for a few seconds.

"Not going to last," Shaylia whispered.

I crowded close, pressing her down against Ethan's chest. "Think you can take us both, Shay?" I asked against the shell of her ear, rubbing my dick along Ethan's as he pulled out.

"Mmm," she agreed, pushing back onto him again.

"Hold still, Ethan," I said, sitting up and positioning my dick against his at her opening. "Breathe, Shay," I murmured, pushing in.

"Oh God," she gasped as I breached, stretching her tight little hole for both of us. "God." She groaned as I pushed in further, the lube easing my way.

Ethan cradled her face and kissed her, and I took my time working my way inside her pussy alongside him, teeth clenched to keep from blowing too soon.

I stared where she stretched, watching my dick disappear into her body with Ethan—right where we belonged.

"Fuck," I whispered, once I bottomed out.

Shaylia shivered between us as I planked and pulled out to the tip.

"Pull out, Ethan," I said through clenched teeth and pushed in when he obeyed my command.

"Oh *God*!" Shaylia climaxed immediately, cum gushing around our dicks, her body convulsing, but we kept a slow, steady pace, drawing every spasm from her pussy. "So good, so full." She panted and squirmed as we continued taking turns fucking in and out of her with teeth-clenching drags that rolled my eyes back into my head.

Finally, she stilled with a heavy sigh, and I leaned down to capture Ethan's mouth. He grasped at my back with bruising fingers, and I wondered at his control.

"More," Shaylia whispered although she lay lax between us.

"Don't want to hurt you, baby," Ethan said with a groan.

"You won't. Take what you want, what you need. Please."

I certainly didn't need to be asked twice. I thrust harder, deeper.

She moaned.

Ethan did the same as I pulled out—the green light since I *knew* she truly wanted us both. Thank fuck for empathic abilities. The scent of sex and vanilla filled my nose as I let loose, giving her what she wanted, taking what I needed.

Her soft flesh jiggled between us, her muffled moans in Ethan's neck spurring me on. I lost myself in her heat, in pure euphoria, having her tight hold grasping both of us together.

"Gonna come," I managed and thrust in so damn hard, Ethan cursed.

We both jerked against her womb at the same time, our cum spurting together, filling her.

Planked over them, my head tipped down as I heaved for breath, my dick twitching with one last drop of cum. "Goddamn," I moaned.

"What a way to wake up," Shaylia said, all dreamy and happy-sounding.

I pulled out, and she sighed, holding tight to Ethan.

"Don't move," I murmured before hurrying to the bathroom. They'd rolled onto their sides but remained connected when I returned, so I spooned against Shaylia's backside.

She sighed as I ran my hand down her side, kissing her shoulder. "You okay?"

"As long as I'm between you two, I'll always be okay," she murmured.

I caught Ethan's gaze and smiled, knowing he felt what I did—complete and utter happiness, as though I could conquer the world as long as I had both of my lovers beside me.

THE END

About the Author

USA Today bestselling author Lynn Burke is a CrossFit and coffee addict. Her three spawn and two fur babies dictate how often she can be found hunched over her Mac, typing as fast as her fickle muse cooks up hot stories.

You can find more about Lynn at her website: www. authorlynnburke.com

Also By Lynn Burke

Abel's Obsession

Divulging Secrets

Healing Storms

In Between

Reluctant Lumberjack

Resisting his Mate

The Playboy Bachelor

Billion Dollar Love Anthology

Blood Born Series

Bonds of Worship Series

Dark Leopards MC

Darkest Desires Series

Devil's Outlaws MC

Elite Escort Series

Fallen Gliders MC

Forbidden Obsession Duet

Found by Fate Series

Midnight Sun Series

Missing Link Series

Risso Family Series

Sandy Ridge Series

Sinful Nature Series

Vicious Vipers MC

www.ingramcontent.com/pod-product-compliance
Lightning Source LLC
Chambersburg PA
CBHW060854210726
48293CB00006B/1792